About the Author

Frank Dirscherl (b. 1973) is the author and editor of the Amazon bestselling *The Wraith* and *Beyond the Lens*. His series of *The Wraith Adventures* books have been enjoyed by multitudes of readers the world over. Other books in the series include *Valley of Evil, Crossfire, Cult of the Damned* and *Cry of the Werewolf,* with more to come.

A professionally certified library technician, who has been working in libraries for over twenty five years, Frank has also worked at a medical practice in a data entry position, covered books for a book wholesale company, as a lecturer to children on the merits, and writing, of comic books, and as an online activist for social equality.

He lives on the south coast of New South Wales, Australia, with his beautiful wife Jennifer, where he is currently working on his latest piece of fiction.

For more information on Frank Dirscherl, please visit his website at **www.frankdirscherl.com**

Praise for *The Wraith*
Amazon bestseller

"I love the coloring job and specially the 'glowing' eyes on the chest of the character."
- Guillermo del Toro, director, *Blade II, Hellboy I & II*

"I liked the story a lot... It's a very strong debut."
Steve Englehart, writer, *Detective Comics, The Avengers, Green Lantern*

"I have read the novel (I couldn't put it down)... It is amazing to see how her (Leena) character evolves from Part I to Part II. At first she appears as every other 'girlfriend' in an action film, but those twelve months that pass obviously change her as a person and I love the person she becomes: tougher, but still human."
- Amber Moelter, actress, *Catwoman: Copycat*

"I finished *The Wraith* book last night. I must say I enjoyed it quite a bit. The scenes kept playing in my head like a big budget Hollywood film. I mentioned earlier that I enjoy when the hero is put to the test physically and doesn't win the battle unscathed. Boy, (Frank) delivered that in spades!"
- Jeff Welborn, artist, *Nightmare World, The Wraith*

"Genius + sweat + dedication = hard hittin' hero action! Go Aussie!"
- Dan Lennard, writer, *People* magazine

"*The Wraith* is a wonderful throwback to the purple prose of the bloody pulps with a hero clearly descendant from the likes of the Shadow and the Spider. A fast, action-packed thrill-ride with great characters, both noble and villainous. Slam-bang kick off to a super new series. One I'm anxious to follow."

> – Ron Fortier, writer, *The Spider, Brother Bones, Domino Lady*

"I became familiar with Frank Dirscherl's The Wraith from the comic book of the same name. When the first Wraith novel came out I just had to read it. I was not disappointed. The Wraith is a fast-paced thrill-ride. I'm looking forward to the upcoming sequel."

> – Bobby Nash, writer, *Evil Ways, Fantastix, Lance Star*

"*The Wraith* (is) a really fun read. Have been a fan of Kenneth Robeson's Doc Savage and The Avenger books for years... *The Wraith* reminds me of Robeson at his best."

> – G.R. Lawson, Publisher, General Jinjur Comics

"A short, pulp, superhero novel... Clearly more adventures to come with how this is set up."

> – Richard Scott, *Super Reader* website

"*The Wraith* is an enlightening journey into the darkness of superhero fiction, and a worthy entry into both pulpdom and comicdom."

> – Kevin Noel Olson, *Silver Bullet Comics* website

"*The Wraith* is a testament to Frank's dedication and talent. Other small press characters have come and gone, but The Wraith endures, because Frank understands what makes a classic character."
  – Richard Evans, writer, *The Canadian Legion*

"When it comes to superhero fiction and classic pulp stories, Frank Dirscherl channels those classic adventures of the past into *The Wraith* with ease and gives you a hero to believe in."
  – Stephen J. Semones, writer/director, *Beyond the Lens, Crossfire, The Wraith: Eyes of Judgment*

"Frank Dirscherl's writing is action-packed and reminds me why superhero fiction is so much fun in the first place!"
  – A.P. Fuchs, writer, *The Axiom-man Saga, The Way of the Fog, Undead World trilogy*

"Totally enjoyed this book. Good story, a real hero vs villain yarn. Can't wait to read the other adventures of The Wraith."
  – J. Newey, *Amazon*

Praise for *Valley of Evil*

"The second Wraith novel is an improvement, I think. Right from the start Dirscherl throws you into the middle of crazy action.... This book is a whole lot of superheroic pulp fun, and the good news is there seems to be more to come...I look forward to some more of the same."

    – Richard Scott, *Super Reader* website

"I think (Dirscherl) really captured a noir element with (his) voice."

    – Joshua Gamon, writer, *Abigail & Rox, Digital Webbing Presents*

"I did quite enjoy the books. Best of all, it wasn't overly sex-filled or gory—I can't stand most modern superhero comics that show such things or have the heroes just swear and swear. So *The Wraith* (and *Valley of Evil*) was just up my alley."

    – Greg Gick, writer, *The Werewolf of Rutherford Grange, Tales of the Shadowmen, Secret Agent X Vol. 2*

"The Dread Avenger is back. After battling the Cobra in his first prose adventure, The Wraith returns to face all new challenges from Metro City's greatest villains, most notably Hong Kong drug kingpin Ma Tzi. As with his first Wraith novel, Frank Dirscherl treats us to a pulp-inspired adventure that keeps readers on the edge of their seat. You have to read this novel in one sitting."

    – Bobby Nash, writer, *Evil Ways, Fantastix, Lance Star*

"In the past five years there has been a tremendous resurgence in pulp fiction centering on the old heroic pulps. Young writers have started taking up the mantle of old masters like Walter Gibson and Lester Dent and begun creating their own avengers in tales of genuine purple prose. Among the best of this new generation of wordsmiths is Australian, Frank Dirscherl and the exploits of his modern pulp paladin, The Wraith. This is grand pulp!"

– Ron Fortier, writer, *The Spider, Brother Bones, Domino Lady*

Praise for *Crossfire*

"Stephen did a fantastic job of bringing Frank Dirscherl's character to life!"
-   Adam DiTroia, composer, *The Wraith: Eyes of Judgment*,
MTV, Fox Sports

"Loved the book!! Can't wait for the next installment..."
-   Larry Mainland, actor, *The Walking Dead, Lawless,
The Three Stooges*

"The action comes swift, and doesn't stop until the final pages. *Crossfire* tells a great story of betrayal and revenge."
-   C.R. Blevins, writer, *A Western Tale*

"This was my first introduction to The Wraith and I was not disappointed. The action comes swift, and doesn't stop until the final pages.... If you love a good action/hero story, you will certainly enjoy reading *Crossfire*."

-   Ally, *Amazon*

"Makes me want more...should be the next series on Netflix..."

-   Bill Lancaster, *Amazon*

Praise for *Cult of the Damned*

"Only by the first three pages, Frank Dirscherl wonderfully captures a dark and mysterious atmosphere, one that leaves the reader with a cryptic and eerie sensation; one that makes me cold just thinking about it."

- Rennie Cowan, writer/director, *The Thriller Idol: A Tribute to the Legacy of Michael Jackson, Kade the Conqueror*

"Frank Dirscherl pulls you into the world of The Wraith from the first sentence and refuses to let you go until the last one."

- Stephen J. Semones, writer/director, *Beyond the Lens, Crossfire, The Wraith: Eyes of Judgment*

"The Wraith is one of my favorite characters and every time Frank Dirscherl puts pen to paper I know I'm in for a real treat."

- A.P. Fuchs, writer, *The Axiom-man Saga, The Way of the Fog, Undead World trilogy*

Praise for *Zombies Attack!* in *Metahumans vs the Undead*

"This compilation of superheroes vs evil offers top entertainment for superhero lovers! Frank Dirscherl and others are at their best with their contributed stories. I will now pursue other stories written by these authors, such as those involving Mr. Dirscherl's The Wraith. This type of reading enjoyment knows no end!"

    –   Ramona Wingart, writer, *Where is Brother Beaver?*, *Emily Suzanne Smith!*

Praise for *Werewolves Attack!* in *Metahumans vs Werewolves*

"Always a great read. Can never put it down once you get started... "

– Geraldine L. Lewis, Amazon

BY FRANK DIRSCHERL

FICTION

The Wraith Adventures series

Sanderson of Metro (with Bobby Nash)
Serpent Rising (with Greg Gick) – COMING SOON
The Wraith
Valley of Evil
Crossfire (by Stephen J. Semones)
Cult of the Damned
Cry of the Werewolf
Vendetta

SHORT STORY COLLECTIONS

Metahumans vs. the Undead
Metahumans vs. Werewolves
Metahumans vs. Robots
Metahumans vs. the Ultimate Evil
Lance Star – Sky Ranger Vol. 1

NON-FICTION

The Wraith: Eyes of Judgment – The Official Script Book & Movie Guide
(with Stephen J. Semones)
The Hitchers of Oz
Beyond the Lens (edited)

COMIC BOOKS

The Wraith #0
The Wraith: The Collected Editions #1-3
The Wraith Books of Judgment Book One
Curse of the Cortes Stone (with Joe Martino & Scott Story)
Shadowflame: Bombed (with Joe Martino)

www.trinitycomics.com

VENDETTA

The Wraith Adventures #5

by

Frank Dirscherl

TRINITY COMICS
WOLLONGONG

TRINITY COMICS
PO Box 31
Wollongong NSW 2520

ISBN 978-0-646-98462-9

PUBLISHED BY TRINITY COMICS, March 2018
www.trinitycomics.com
COVER LAYOUT AND DESIGN AND INTERIOR DESIGN by Frank Dirscherl
EDITED by AP Fuchs

For more on *Vendetta*
visit www.trinitycomics.com

Text set in Garamond-Normal. Printed and bound in the USA

NATIONAL
LIBRARY
OF AUSTRALIA

A catalogue record for this book is available from the National Library of Australia

The Wraith Adventures series in correct reading order (including short stories)

So far...

The story goes on...

* The novels *Sanderson of Metro* and *Serpent Rising* take place partially in the past and partially in the present, hence their multiple listings above.

For my loving wife and family, as always

~ Chapter 1 ~

Robert Latham strode into the ornately designed and furnished study in his Metro City home and moved over to the deep mahogany sideboard and poured himself a Cognac from the crystal decanter there. He sniffed, drank, and gazed around the room. Decorated in much the same fashion as his city office, there were duplicate busts of the world leaders throughout history that he so admired. For their strength, their cunning. Their ruthlessness. Caesar, Genghis Khan, Stalin, Mao Ze Dong, George W. Bush and Donald Trump were but some of the specimens there. He took another drink, the delicious Remy Martin warming his throat and clarifying his thoughts. He headed to his desk.

Taking a seat in the plush buttoned leather chair, he hadn't even a moment to relax before the phone rang.

"Yes?" he said indignantly. "Oh, Patrich. Good of you to call. What news?"

He took another sip from his drink, savoring the taste while listening.

"You've dealt with that arriviste Jones, then? Excellent. Oh dear, another deputy with delusions of grandeur. At least Charlie had some sense of patience, and bided his time before trying anything. I spared Charlie for that reason. He may not have been loyal but at least he was halfway competent. But Jones...he never had a chance." Latham leaned back in his chair and smiled. "You're not going to get any similar ideas now are you, Patrich? I wouldn't be very pleased to have to do away with three deputies in a row. My reputation would take a battering." He paused. "Good, smart boy. Good work tonight, also. Efficient and deadly. Traits I admire. You can go home now. We have a busy day tomorrow."

He hung up before any response could be received.

Leaning forward, he chuckled briefly while reaching for the alabaster cigar case on his desk. As he opened the lid and reached inside, the light instantly dimmed to almost nothing, and a screen dropped down from the ceiling at the far end of the room.

"What the...?"

"Now, now," a familiar voice emanated seemingly from nowhere and everywhere all at once.

"Charlie?" Latham said, with a mixture of bemusement and anger. "How the he—?"

"Temper, temper," Charlie Grieco said as his face flashed upon the large screen. Latham's former deputy appeared always the same: slickly dressed with a smarmy, arrogant air about him. "Is that any way to greet your old comrade?" He laughed while talking.

"What's going on here, Charlie? How did you get this stuff in here?"

Grieco grinned. "Can the great Robert Latham have forgotten that I was his right-hand man for nearly ten years? That I know all his secrets, inside and out?"

"I changed every passcode, altered all my security procedures as I always do after every..." Latham wheezed.

"Purge?" Grieco chimed in. "Is that how you were about to explain your betrayal of me?"

Latham fumed. "Betrayal of you? You little worm! You tried to usurp control of my organization for yourself. Thought yourself the new big man of Metro City."

"Because you wouldn't let go!" Grieco screamed. "You didn't know when to step aside and let some fresh blood taste their fair share of power. You delayed me from my destiny. And now it's going to cost you."

Latham recovered his composure, leaned back, and lit his cigar, blowing smoke before continuing. "Cost me? You must be insane. I don't know where you are or how you managed to pull this off, but you're a dead man, you hear me. A dead man!"

"Funny," Grieco replied, his smile never leaving him, "I was thinking the same thing about you. You asked before how I managed to achieve my little show for you in your study there. Well, I can't take all the credit, you know. I had a little bit of help. I bumped into an old friend of ours, you see. With my knowledge of your practices, and his...well, skills...we were able to..."

"Get to the point, Charlie," Latham snapped.

"Hmm...well, why don't I let him tell you about it, then."

Grieco stepped out of camera range and was quickly replaced by another man, one Latham knew all too well. Crossfire!

He's alive, Latham thought, genuinely frightened for the first time in his life. *How is this possible?*

His tall, muscular frame filled the screen with an imposing menace. His long blond hair was in a ponytail just like it was the last time they had met, and there was that annoying little cross-hairs tattoo on the left side of his neck, but he appeared different as well, outfitted in a formfitting black bodysuit, with bullet pouches crisscrossing both shoulders. Emblazoned at the top of his chest was a small duplicate image of the tattoo, in white, with a smeared, blood-red center dot. As the villain leaned in close to the camera, his heavily-tanned and lined face became clearer.

"Latham...by your expression I see you remember me," Crossfire said.

Latham found it difficult to breathe. Charlie Grieco and Crossfire teaming up, somehow able to penetrate the security of his home.

"You're no doubt wondering how I come to be alive, how and why I've teamed up with our mutual friend here," he said, gesturing off camera. "The why I'm sure you can work out for yourself. As to the first question...you're going to take that one unanswered to your grave."

Latham gulped, sweat pouring down his brow. He tried to move but was paralyzed with fear, a feeling completely alien to him. "But, but...my family, don't..."

Grieco re-appeared on the screen to stand alongside the much larger Crossfire, the latter of which produced a small apparatus from his belt.

"Goodbye," Crossfire breathed, while Grieco cackled, pressing a button on the apparatus.

A burst of fiery light shot forth, and then...

Darkness.

* * * * * *

The Latham mansion exploded in an inferno that was almost akin to a nuclear detonation. In seconds, the massive house was reduced to mere rubble, and flames spewed skyward as though the devil's domain was attempting an invasion of Heaven itself. In minutes, with the sirens of the emergency crews sounding in the distance, the conflagration grew, spreading throughout the grounds of the estate. There was no stopping it.

Crossfire's vengeance had been complete. And satisfied.

*　*　*　*　*　*

Grieco couldn't contain his joy. He shrieked and danced about like a nerd prancing at the prom with the head cheerleader.

"I did it," he shouted. "He's gone. The old man is finally history, and I'm free to take over the organization. Finally to lead."

He turned to face his newfound ally. Crossfire stared back at him with a stern expression belying any joy he might have felt at their success.

"Why so glum?" Grieco said, oblivious to anything other than his own ecstasy. "Your enemy is dead. Your mission is complete. Now you can go home to Cobar, or wherever it was you said you came from. Unless, of course, you want a job in *my* organization. I could use a man with your...skills."

Crossfire remained motionless, merely staring at Grieco for some further seconds before finally speaking. "You think my mission is over? That killing Latham is all that I desire?"

"Well, I...I don't know, I..." Grieco said, finally starting to think the situation might not be quite as he imagined. He took a few steps back.

"Latham was just the beginning," Crossfire barked. "And you were simply a means to an end. And now it is *your* end."

Grieco gulped. Crossfire lifted a gauntleted arm, smirked, and fired.

* * * * * *

Lead coughed from the miniature automatic weapon secreted within the fabric of the arm of Crossfire's suit. A powerful Uzi-style weapon, it connected with the bullets strapped around his bulky frame, meaning it unlikely he would ever run out of bullets in the short term.

The barrage of bullets tore Grieco's body to shreds. When Crossfire finally relented, bloody pieces of flesh were strewn at his feet. He didn't care. As he had said—a means to an end. All his enemies would suffer the same fate. However, Grieco's remains, and Latham's demise, would send a message to the one enemy he was *really* after. The one who deserved every torture, every cruelty, and then finally, death, more than any other.

The Wraith.

~ Chapter 2 ~

KARBAH, IRAQ - SIX MONTHS EARLIER

The sun beat down on his forehead as he guided the plow through the dusty field on the outskirts of the border town. The oxen ahead of him grunted and groaned with the exertion in the heat of the day, but Crossfire, outfitted in a simple tank top and cargo pants, matched the creature for effort in every way. He had been in Karbah ever since his aborted attempts at revenge upon Metro City crime lord Robert Latham some time back. He had returned to this village—after his failure—to regroup, to gather his strength...and maybe to find a little bit of his soul once again. Karbah had been where he had last felt like himself, truly alive, with his comrades in Devil Company. It was as close to a place he might call home as anywhere on the planet. He was only too relieved the village had thus far stayed out of the line of fire of ISIL or anyone else looking for a fight. The last thing he needed right now was another war.

Pausing briefly to wipe his brow, he was about to urge the beast to continue when a young man called out behind him, begging his attention.

"Mr. Thomas," the young man shouted in Arabic. "Mr. Thomas, sir."

"I told you not to call me that," Crossfire sternly replied, also in Arabic. "My name is Crossfire, now and forevermore."

"A thousand apologies, Mr. Crossfire," the young man said, bowing, "but Namatullah said you would want to know."

"Know? Know what?"

The young man smiled and looked eager to please, but said nothing. Crossfire knew the lad hero-worshiped him to a degree, but this was the first time he had seen the evidence of it first-hand. To a degree was putting it mildly.

"Speak up!" Crossfire barked.

"The newspapers have arrived," the young man said. "There is news. Namatullah says you have to read the news."

"It can't be that important," Crossfire said, about to ready the plow once again. Since returning to the village, he had worked hard, day in, day out, helping at any task that was required. "It can wait until I've finished."

"No, Mr. Crossfire. Namatullah says it is about Metro City. In America."

That did it. The mere mention of that haven of sin prompted Crossfire to act. Whatever it was, clearly Namatullah thought it important enough to send the lad out to get him. Metro City. He had to know what was going on.

Crossfire dropped the plow into the dirt and rushed back toward the village.

* * * * * *

Late into the night, the catastrophe was finally under control, with only a small amount of spot fires some distance from the blast zone still to be dealt with. Amongst the army of fire fighters and other emergency personnel, crime scene investigators were on-site, carefully sifting through the rubble, trying to make sense of the disaster. Watching on were Detectives Bob Sloan and his partner Rosa Perez. Sloan paced back and forth, as was his wont, outfitted in his usual jeans, T-shirt and baseball cap. As Sloan glanced up at her, Perez gave him that distinct look he had come to know well over the many years of their partnership on the force. Sloan and Perez were one of the good guys, one of the few incorruptible officers Metro City had, though Commissioner George Harrison was slowly dealing with that particular problem.

"What is it this time, Perez?" Sloan asked.

"Just you," she replied. "How you always pace up and down when something bothers you." Perez was much more professionally attired in a tidy blouse and pressed pants, her long, straight black hair swept up in a simple ponytail. Her no-nonsense demeanor, though, did little to hide her feminine qualities.

"Well, look at this place," he said, gesticulating around him, "there's nothing left. We're told by Latham's office he was working from home tonight, and then all hell breaks loose here."

"Rival gang hit?" Perez probed. "Ma Tzi's organization coming back for more, perhaps? Or a new player on the scene? I don't suppose this could have been an accident. Perhaps a gas leak or some such."

"Nah," Sloan said, shaking his head. "His gang died with him. And I doubt a gas leak could achieve this much damage. New player? Maybe. But my gut says this is something bigger, something...much worse..."

A skinny, superbly dressed man approached them. The man gingerly tread over the wreckage that had once been the Latham home. No doubt he didn't want to ruin his shiny black leather shoes, Sloan thought.

"Excuse me, Mr...?" Sloan started.

"Patrich Azufi," the man quickly replied. "Mr. Latham's close business associate."

"Ah, you mean chief stooge," Sloan shot back with some venom. "Head flunky to the big man. That explains what you're doing here."

"How dare you," Azufi spat before quickly regaining his composure, smoothing his hands down his fine, grey flannel suit.

Sloan eyed him carefully. From his greasy, bolt-upright-but-thinning hair to his carefully manicured nails, Azufi gave the impression of a poseur, a mighty egotist. The words sleazy and smug came instantly to mind, but somehow they weren't quite adequate.

"Rather than hurl insults," Azufi said, "I would have hoped you'd be doing your jobs and finding out who was responsible for this outrage."

"Give us time, Mr. Azufi," Perez said, ever the diplomat. "We need time to do our jobs properly."

"Time?" Azufi snapped. Feigning outrage, Sloan thought. "Time? Robert Latham and his family have been slaughtered, and all you're doing is lollygagging about. I'll have words with the commissioner about this. The mayor."

"You go do that," Sloan said. "Feel free to join the queue. In the meantime, I'd appreciate you getting outta my face and letting me get back to my work. Comprendé?"

Sloan turned and marched a few steps toward the CSI technicians, leaving Perez and Azufi alone behind him.

"How're we doing, Jim?" Sloan asked as he crouched down beside the head of the CSI division.

Before Jim could answer, Sloan turned and glanced back at his partner trying to placate Azufi. The latter stared back with daggers in his eyes, an expression that would have been more effective, Sloan thought, if Azufi was not affecting such a strange, stiff, side-ward pose, as though he was a comic book superhero obsessed with his own image in the mirror.

"Too early to say too much," Jim began, "but we've already found some human remains and evidence of some sort of accelerant used. Whoever was in the house, nobody could have survived this. Anything we find, we'll bag it and take it back to the lab."

"Good. Keep at it."

Sloan stood and was joined by Perez, who had seen the chagrined Azufi off the premises. "Human remains, Perez. No survivors."

"So this is it," Perez said. "Accident or not, this *is* it. The end of an era. Robert Latham is truly gone."

Sloan furrowed his brow. "Why does that not comfort me, Perez? Why does that not comfort me?"

* * * * * *

With the wind curling his cape around him, The Wraith lowered his long-range binoculars, then snapped them back onto his belt. From his vantage point atop a nearby skyscraper, he had witnessed the carnage wrought on the Latham home by some unknown agent, and watched Bob Sloan and Rosa Perez on the scene. But he needed more information, and fast. He pressed at a point on his temple, activating his in-cowl radio.

"Max. Do you have anything?"

"Not yet, Chief, apart from the obvious," The Wraith's right-hand man Max Horton said with his usual Irish brogue. "Some sort of attack on the Latham mansion. Took out not only the main house but pretty much the entire estate."

"I can confirm that," The Wraith said. "Any word on survivors?"

"From what I can gather from what the police are saying, Robert Latham worked from home tonight. So, if that's true, and whomever else was there at the time...they're all dead."

The Wraith tightly set his jaw. Someone was declaring war on the Latham organization. On Latham himself. And had possibly taken the man out as a result. The Wraith's greatest nemesis—gone. The thought brought him no joy, only a strong feeling of unease. War had been declared, that was true. But not only on Robert Latham and his criminal empire, but on Metro City itself.

And that was a war The Wraith was unwilling to allow to continue.

* * * * * *

KARBAH, IRAQ - SIX MONTHS EARLIER

Crossfire charged into the small abode, the timber door loudly bashing against the wall, causing the inhabitant to jump with surprise.

"Mr. Crossfire, sir. You startled me," the elder man said.

"What's this about Metro City, Namatullah? In the newspaper?"

Namatullah smiled, his yellow teeth coming into view. He was quite old, though Crossfire could never discern just how old. He was considered one of the village's elder statesmen. Wise and just, he was the closest thing to a friend Crossfire had.

"Yes, the papers have come in from America. You wanted me to let you know if Metro City was ever mentioned, and," Namatullah said, reaching for a newspaper from an adjacent table, "here it is."

Crossfire snatched it from the old man's hands, not delaying with any niceties. The paper, the *Metro City Times*, was already two months old, but clearly Namatullah thought it contained something of value.

"Page five, sir."

Crossfire almost tore the pages to get there, but the headline stood out once he arrived:

METRO CITY BUSINESSMAN ARRESTED ON DRUG AND WEAPONS TRAFFICKING CHARGES

So, Crossfire thought, *the underling finally made a move but was outsmarted either by his boss or The Wraith. Possibly both. Interesting.*

After some minutes, Crossfire laid the paper down and smiled.

Grieco's arrest...I can use this situation to my advantage. This is what I've been waiting for. It's time to return to Metro City.

~ Chapter 3 ~

The Wraith strode into the Lair, removed his cowl, and plunked himself down at his computer terminal. With a few taps of the keys, files on Robert Latham popped up on the three large screens facing him. Everything on Latham The Wraith had—his business dealings, both legal and illegal; his past; his relationships; everything that was known about the crime lord appeared onscreen.

The electric door on the floor above whirred open, but apart from vaguely hearing it, The Wraith paid it no close attention.

"Darling?" Leena's voice sounded as The Wraith heard her descend to the Lair's main floor in the small, egg-shaped open elevator. "Max told me the news. Robert Latham is dead?"

"That's what the police believe, but I'm not so sure."

"You doubt the reports?" Leena said, her long, strawberry-blonde hair bouncing about as she walked.

"Human remains were found, granted, but there's no proof yet they were Latham's. His wife was known to be home, and there would no doubt be a bevy of servants as well." He rubbed his chin with consternation. "I just don't think Latham could be taken out quite so easily."

"Perhaps you're over-thinking things," Leena said, placing an arm over his broad shoulders. "You've done that a lot lately ever since Dr. Satanish perished more than six months ago."

"I know, I know," he replied with a sigh, "but I can't help it. I just have this gut feeling about Satanish, and if he could get away under similar circumstances, I don't see why Latham couldn't have as well."

"Let's wait and see what the lab boys have to say."

The Wraith swiveled in his chair. "There's no need to wait. After Sloan and Perez left the scene, I managed to sneak my way there and come away with some samples of my own." He patted at his belt to highlight the point. "Max will be able to come up with an analysis faster than the police could."

"Did someone say my name," Max called out from the upper level, the door having just opened to reveal his presence.

"Samples to be analyzed," The Wraith said. "Possible human remains. I need to know if they might be Robert Latham's, and I need to know as soon as possible."

* * * * * *

MELTON MEMORIAL INTERNATIONAL AIRPORT – TWO MONTHS EARLIER

Crossfire, in civilian attire and carrying two hefty duffel bags, marched out of Melton Memorial, Metro City's international airport, and briefly looked up at the immense city skyline, blazing in the early evening, ahead in the distance. He hadn't anticipated returning to Metro quite this soon, but opportunity waited for no man, as the cliché went. He made for the nearest cab in the rank.

"Where you headed, buddy?" the cab driver hollered.

Crossfire dumped his luggage in the trunk, then joined the driver upfront. "The nearest cheap hotel."

"How cheap?" the driver asked, raising an eyebrow.

"*Cheap*," Crossfire said.

"You got it. Pembleton it is."

As the cab sped through the outer boroughs, the driver began to regale his passenger with all sorts of questions and tales. All the while Crossfire remained still and silent.

"Where you from, buddy?" the driver asked.

Silence.

"Back home from a trip?"

No reply.

"How long you been away?"

Nothing.

"Me," the driver continued, ignoring the lack of response from his passenger, "I've never been overseas. The missus and me have never even left Metro City. Why would you want to leave this place? See the world? You got the whole world right here. I ain't ever had a need to go anywhere else."

Crossfire turned and stared briefly at the pudgy driver, the latter's stubbly and pockmarked face a standout feature.

"Am I wrong?" the driver said. At a red light, he looked over to Crossfire and began to stare. "Say, don't I know you?" He lurched as he almost lost control of the cab in the traffic.

"I never forget a face. It's a useful habit to have as a cabbie. Now, don't tell me, don't tell me."

As the light turned green, the driver gunned the car forward. After some little time winding their way through city traffic, the vehicle finally arrived at its destination: a flea bag hotel known as the Pembleton Arms.

"Here you are, buddy. The cheapest you'll ever find."

Crossfire remained still, facing forward.

"I do know you, you're..." Crossfire looked over, saw the trepidation on the driver's face as recognition set in.

"Is there a back entrance?" Crossfire asked softly.

"Umm...yeah. There's a parking lot out back."

"Take me there."

"Sure, sure," the driver said nervously.

Rounding the dilapidated building, the cab came to a stop in the near-deserted, and poorly lit, hotel parking lot.

"You...you want some help with your bags?" the driver asked.

Crossfire remained still once again, staying silent for a few moments before finally speaking. "Unfortunately for you, you somehow recognized me. Nobody must know I'm here. Not yet."

In a lightning-fast move, he reached across, grabbed the cabbie's head and twisted violently, snapping the hapless driver's neck as though it was a twig.

Casually exiting the cab, Crossfire removed his luggage from the trunk, then carefully placed the body there. There was no one around to bear witness to the crime.

Looking up at the rear entrance of the crumbling abode, he clutched a bag in each hand and trudged up the stairs to the door.

* * * * * *

The sun began to cast ominous shadows across the main precinct of the Metro City Police Headquarters as dawn broke. Detective Perez strolled into the station, thinking she might just have beaten Sloan into the office for once, but wasn't overly surprised to find her partner already there at his desk.

"Geez, Bob, don't you ever go home?"

"Isn't this home?" he replied, only half-joking.

"Why your wife stays with you, I'll never know."

"Natural charm," Sloan said with a twinkle in his eye, "plus devastating good looks."

"Oh boy," Perez said, rolling her eyes. "Any news?"

"Still too early for anything definitive, but I think we can safely say the Latham family may now be extinct."

"Sloan! Perez! In my office *now*!" a familiar voice boomed.

Sloan looked over to Perez. They knew what was coming.

"Don't bother sitting down," Commissioner Harrison said as they entered his office. "You won't be here that long."

"Let me guess," Sloan said. "This Azufi guy has made a complaint, either to you or higher up. And you're about to give us the obligatory dressing down as a result."

"Don't be a wise guy," Harrison said, hands on hips. "We have proper procedures that must always be followed."

"Give me a break. That guy was in my face, Commish. Trying to tell us how to do our jobs. I won't stand for that sort of crap."

"You'll stand for what I tell you to stand for, Sloan," Harrison lectured. "I'm only now finally making some headway in cleaning up this department. I need to stay in the mayor's office's good books to be able to continue the job."

Perez looked over to her partner, noting his exasperated expression.

"You two are good cops," Harrison continued. "Two of my very best. I just need you to be careful right now. I haven't yet figured out our new mayor yet. The politics right now are very delicate. We all have to tread very cautiously for the present. I need you guys with me on this."

"Yes, sir," Perez said. "C'mon, Bob, let's get back to work."

She grabbed Sloan by the right arm and practically dragged him away.

"I want your report on this explosion on my desk by midday," Harrison called out.

Sloan raised his thumb and sat back at his desk.

"We need to do something while we wait for forensics to possibly give us some sort of lead," Perez said.

"Just what I was thinking. You stay here and write up the report for ole grumpy, while I head over to Latham HQ and interview some of the people there."

"Oh no," Perez said, placing her head in her hands. "You heard what the Commissioner just said."

"Don't worry," Sloan said, grabbing his coat from the back of his chair, a broad grin on his face, "I'll be discretion itself. Ever the diplomat."

"Yeah, right."

"Trust me, Perez. Trust me."

* * * * * *

METRO CITY - TWO MONTHS EARLIER

Crossfire laid back on the propped up pillows on his hotel room bed. A roach scurried about on the far wall, but he paid it little attention. His mind was churning as he tried to formulate his plans for revenge and power. He needed some sort of home-base and equipment before proceeding further. Transportation had been taken care of, at least temporarily, but he'd need to replace the cab soon. Once he had everything he needed, and everything solidified in his mind, only then could he go ahead with the next stage.

Break Charlie Grieco out of jail.

~ Chapter 4 ~

Sloan parked his ramshackle Buick at the front of the impressive Latham Industries building. Still the tallest structure in Metro, the roof featured a giant letter L logo atop it to ensure everyone in the city knew that the name Latham did indeed start with the letter L.

A burly man in his fifties, Sloan jumped up the building's steps two-at-a-time, bumping briefly into someone, before entering through the spinning, glass circular door.

"Detective Bob Sloan," he announced at the front desk, flashing his badge in the young receptionist's face. "Investigating last night's incident at the Latham home." He briefly looked around the stunning glass and marble lobby before continuing. "I need to see Mr. Latham's agenda for the past few weeks and I'd like to speak to his close associates as well. Can you arrange this for me, please?"

He was laying on the charm as best he could, and the young thing—a pretty girl of no more than twenty, Sloan guessed—did her best to acquiesce. She was on the phone in an instant and started blathering away.

While he waited, he again checked out his surroundings. The lobby was modern and clean, polished glass and steel all around them, charcoal marble beneath their feet. Pillars were marble, too, though of a cream tint. This was big money and how. Crime clearly did pay.

"Mr. Azufi will see you now," the receptionist twittered. "He's taking over the business while Mr Latham...while..."

"I'm sure he is," Sloan replied with some sarcasm.

"Joel," the receptionist called out to an assistant, a skinny young man, superbly outfitted as everyone else was in the building, at the far end of the desk, "could you please escort Detective Sloan to Mr. Azufi's office?"

"This way, please," the young man said with a smile, gesturing behind them.

"How are you all coping with the news?" Sloan enquired, trying to get inside his mind to, perhaps, find something that might lead somewhere.

Someone around here might know something of use.

"It's very sad, of course," the young man said, "though we're all holding out hope that Mr. Latham has survived. There's still no concrete proof of his demise, correct?"

"That's right, but I wouldn't hold out too much hope," Sloan said, trying for a reaction. He got none.

They ascended a narrow, spiral staircase that could only be accessed by a locked gate then opened with a swipe card. A few turns and they reached the top.

"This is Azufi's office?" Sloan asked, feeling slightly dizzy.

"This was...is Mr. Latham's new office after the recent refurbishment. He wanted a view of the lobby and out onto the street, so this overhanging floor was built."

"Azufi sure didn't take long to move in on the old man's territory," Sloan said.

The young man showed no signs of agitation. He wasn't falling for Sloan's act. Or he was too square to understand. He knocked on the door and opened it a second later.

"Detective Sloan is here to speak with you, sir."

He then retreated and vanished down the stairs.

Refurbished office, Sloan thought, *but those damn busts are still here*, noting their presence on the far right of the expansive room.

"Detective Sloan," Azufi said, slimy as ever, this time wearing a pinstripe navy suit. "Good to see you again so soon. Come in and sit down." He beckoned to a chair. "No hard feelings after yesterday. The emotion of the situation, you understand."

"Nice office," Sloan said, not being able to help himself. He had to push the envelope.

"Oh, it's not mine." Azufi chuckled. "But I found it difficult to...fill in for Mr. Latham properly from my own office, so I temporarily relocated here."

"Temporarily." Sloan repeated the word with interest. "So you believe Robert Latham is still alive?"

Azufi flashed a nervous sort of smile. "My own personal opinion here is surely irrelevant. To ensure morale remains high within the organization, we're all talking about *when* Mr. Latham returns, not if. At least until we have definite proof to suggest otherwise."

"What *is* your own personal opinion, Mr. Azufi?" Sloan asked, producing a notepad and pen from his pocket.

Azufi leaned forward in his chair, propped his elbows up on the desk, and spoke in a hushed tone. "I don't see how Mr. Latham could have possibly survived. He told me himself yesterday afternoon he was going home early and would do some work there into the early evening."

"And what time in the afternoon did he leave here?"

"Just before four, I think."

"The explosion occurred around seven. Three hours left unaccounted for."

"I don't think Mr. Latham would have gone anywhere else but home after leaving here," Azufi said, still appearing somewhat nervous. "His wife was planning a special dinner she was making herself. She had sent all the servants home. Besides, he was alive just before seven as I spoke to him on the phone at around that time."

"Oh ho," Sloan said, sitting up straight, excitement rising. Now he was getting somewhere. "You didn't mention the phone call before. I'll have to get the phone records to determine the exact time, but I think this is pretty conclusive proof the big man is history."

Azufi winced at that but said nothing.

"What was the phone call about?" Sloan asked.

"Surely that's not relevant?"

"Everything is relevant in a murder investigation."

"Murder?" Azufi gasped. Sloan couldn't tell whether the reaction was truly genuine or not. "But surely it could have been an accident. A gas explosion, perhaps."

"We've found evidence of an accelerant being used. This was no accident."

Azufi stood, scowled and rubbed his chin. He almost looked human for once. "I don't know what to say."

"Then tell me what your phone conversation was about. Did he call you, or..."

"I called him," Azufi quickly answered. "It was merely about some issues in our human resources department that Mr. Latham had asked me to look into. I simply relayed my findings to him."

"And they were?"

"Nothing of consequence to this investigation."

Sloan stood. "We'll see about that." He waited a few seconds. "Do you mind if I speak with other members of the staff?"

"Yes...yes, of course, go right ahead."

Sloan nodded and headed for the door. Before exiting, he turned to face Azufi one last time. "Rest assured, we'll get whoever was responsible for this. I've made it my mission."

Azufi weakly smiled and Sloan left him there with his thoughts.

* * * * * *

"No need for Mr. Latham's diary," Paul Sanderson could hear Sloan say. "I've got all the information I need for now."

Paul watched from his Rolls Royce Wraith Black Badge parked across the street as Sloan exited the Latham Industries building and sped away in his bomb. Paul removed his earpiece and pressed down upon the RR symbol in the steering wheel. The logo lit up and turned a vivid emerald green.

"Yes, Chief?" Max's voice emanated from the speakers a moment later.

"The bug worked perfectly," Paul said. "I bumped into Sloan in front of the Latham building, decided to let him do my investigating for me. He never noticed the bug being placed into his pocket. Max...there's no doubt now...Latham is dead."

Max whistled before speaking. "I have some preliminary results from my tests. We have samples of both male and female DNA, but with no family members of Latham extant, we have nothing to compare these with to get a match. Possibly with his wife and their staff, but I'll need to look into that."

"Hmm...despite what Azufi told Sloan, I see I'll have to make an appearance to express my condolences after all," Paul said. He looked down at his new Tudor Heritage Black Bay Blue watch, which signaled nine-thirty in the morning. "There must be something in Latham's office which has his DNA."

"Good," Max said. "I'll keep at it here and see if there's anything else I can uncover. Out."

Paul took a step out of his car and looked up at the imposing structure before him.

Here goes.

* * * * * *

"Mr. Sanderson, come in," Patrich Azufi purred, greeting him with a seedy smile and a limp handshake. "Please take a seat. I see it's my day for visitors."

Paul, wearing a steel blue Jon DeBoise tailored sport coat over a turtleneck and chinos, smiled in reply. "I can imagine, what with what happened yesterday. You must be flooded with calls and visits."

"Yes, such a tragedy. We shall miss Mr. Latham more than we can say. And poor Sharon, his wife..." He paused. "Yes, the police have been here and, of course, others have expressed their commiserations."

"That's why I'm here," Paul said. "To express my sincerest condolences and best wishes to everyone at Latham Industries. Robert and I weren't close in a business sense, but we mixed socially and, of course, contributed to many of the same charities."

"Good of you to say," Azufi said as he sat at his desk and slightly leaned back. "Mr. Latham always spoke very highly of you to me. Very highly."

Sure, Paul thought, *sure*.

"Well, if that's all," Azufi said since he appeared about to stand up. "It's been a very busy day, and I—"

Paul took a sharp breath. He spotted the projectile hurtling toward the window behind Azufi and instantly acted, yanking the businessman from his chair and, with Azufi in tow, rushed back toward the spiral staircase. As the missile hit, they careened down the stairs, tumbling violently as flames licked down at them.

They fell in a heap at the bottom to be met with screams of abject terror, with people running to and fro in an absolute panic.

Mayhem.

Paul was up quickly, checked to see Azufi was okay, then sprinted for the building exit. Out on the street, traffic was banked up as the realization of an explosion in the building came home to all. Paul tried to edge through the massed crowds in a vain effort to get a better view of the building opposite where the missile had originated. But nothing could be seen.

From where he stood, there was evidence of nothing.

* * * * * *

Crossfire lowered his right arm and disconnected the miniature missile launcher that had been attached there and connected it to his belt instead. He smiled. He knew his enemy hadn't been taken out with that hit, but that hadn't been his intention. Not yet. It was merely a warning. He had other plans to fulfill before achieving his ultimate aim. And he knew he needed to leave quickly before his enemy would come for him.

~ Chapter 5 ~

METRO CITY - TWO MONTHS EARLIER

Crossfire sat at a battered old desk in a darkened warehouse perusing a plethora of information on his laptop. He leaned back and took a deep breath. This was proving more difficult than he thought. He needed weaponry and equipment, and thought it easy to find both in a city like Metro City by researching the Dark Net, but the source had to be just right. Someone reliable, someone discreet, with just the right skill-set.

At that point, he found exactly that.

Lazar, of course! He's the best gunsmith in the world. I thought he had retired, but he's just set up shop here in Metro. He can custom make and supply everything I need.

He stood and cracked his knuckles. He felt the excitement building. The thrill of the hunt was upon him. He didn't realize until then how much he'd missed the sensation, that adrenaline rush. He felt joy then, too, for he knew vengeance would soon be at hand. All those who had betrayed him and his team, and all who stood in his way, would soon be punished.

He ambled around the near deserted building, one of the warehouses he had used in his previous assault on the city. If his cover was ever to be blown, he thought it extremely unlikely anyone would ever consider searching for him here in one of the very buildings he had previously utilized. In his mind, it made for the perfect hideout.

Rubbing at the back of his neck, trying to get the crick out of it, he walked over to the parked taxi cab he had absconded with. He knew it would be too dangerous to continue using it, so his first priority had now become to dispose of it—and the body still hidden within. Once that had been done, and replacement transportation been procured, then he would be ready to pay Señor Lazar a personal visit.

* * * * * *

Fifty-third street was completely barricaded for a three-block radius. Barriers, with armed officers manning them, were in place at each perimeter to ensure nobody could get in —or out—to disturb the emergency crews in their various frantic duties. The wounded were either being escorted out to waiting ambulances on a series of gurneys, or being treated for more minor injuries at the scene by a platoon of paramedics. Firefighters were only just finally dealing with the last of the embers caused by the explosion, and the CSI division of the police force was now arriving.

Paul sat on the bottom step of the stairs leading up to the Latham building, a disheveled Patrich Azufi alongside him. Azufi shivered uncontrollably.

A car screeched to a halt before them, with Commissioner Harrison appearing from the late model saloon. He was quickly met by Bob Sloan and Rosa Perez, who had emerged from the massed throng off to the side, and briefly chatted with their chief before gesturing to Paul.

"Mr. Sanderson." Harrison greeted Paul with a firm handshake. "I understand you're our sole witness to this terrorist attack."

"He saved my life," Azufi blurted in a monotone whisper. "He saved my life."

"It was nothing, really," Paul said, gently patting Azufi on the shoulder. The businessman didn't seem to notice, blankly staring forward. "We'll get you some help."

"This man needs some attention," Harrison bellowed to a nearby paramedic. "Get him to the hospital."

After the pitiful Azufi had been evacuated from the scene, Harrison returned to the conversation at hand. "So, tell me what you saw of this attack?"

Paul squirmed a little. He hated being stuck there. He wanted to be across the street, investigating the scene of the crime, the place from which the missile had been launched, before the police could possibly taint it in their efforts in finding a clue. But his duty to the injured had been clear. He stayed back to help the wounded and keep the situation as calm as possible within the building until help arrived.

"My meeting with Mr. Azufi had just concluded when I saw something through the window coming toward us. It was only an instant, but it looked to me like a small rocket or missile. I stumbled backward, grabbed Azufi to try and keep my balance, and we both fell down the stairs," Paul explained, laying it on thick. He looked up to spot Sloan standing nearby with a sly grin on his face.

"You're both incredibly lucky to still be alive," Harrison said, putting his fingers through his toupee. "You were in the heart of the inferno and you're still alive. I've been told there has been no loss of life to this point, though three are in critical condition. Our forensic team will determine exactly what weapon was used. We'll get to the bottom of this, mark my words."

He placed a reassuring hand on Paul's shoulder and made his way up and into the building. Perez swiftly followed, with Sloan bringing up the rear. He winked and smiled at Paul before passing by.

Hmm... Paul thought. *What was* that *all about?*

As he ruminated on that, he stood and slowly made his way through the crowd toward his parked Rolls, explaining to an officer there he had already given his statement to Commissioner Harrison and was free to go.

Once inside the car, he pressed on the steering wheel RR logo.

"Yes, Chief?" Max said shortly thereafter.

"Conference time," Paul said. "You, Leena, and I have much to discuss. I'll be home as soon as I can. Out."

* * * * * *

METRO CITY CHINATOWN – TWO MONTHS EARLIER

Smoke billowed from both buildings and alleyways. It was a frigid, overcast night; colder than the norm for this time of year. Unlike other such Chinatown's throughout the country and the world, which were meccas for tourists and food lovers alike, Metro's was a filthy cesspool, a haven for gangs, pushers, hookers, and pedophiles. The stench of death hung in the air.

Crossfire, clad in a dark trench coat, his head bowed, trudged down the sidewalk toward his destination. It was late, but the man he wished to see apparently preferred doing business in the late hours. Turning into a narrower side street, he was confronted by a group of young Asian punks. They looked like they meant business. They had no idea who they were dealing with.

"Well, well. Look at this," the one with the mohawk said, a glint in his eye. "You're a pretty one."

"Look at his luscious hair," another said. "We got a pretty boy here."

"He's got some muscles, too," a third said, this one outfitted in leather and chains. "A pretty boy who works out."

"Is that right, pretty boy? You like to work out?" Mohawk said.

The four punks moved to surround their intended prey. Crossfire remained still and silent, his head still slightly bowed.

"I like the strong, silent type," the fourth of the group finally spoke. By his appearance and demeanor, Crossfire estimated he was their leader. "That's just *my* type."

The leader took a few steps forward, attempted to plant a sloppy one on Crossfire, but never came even close. Crossfire reached forward with his right arm and in a lightning-fast move, grabbed the leader tightly by the throat and squeezed with all his might. The leader, now held aloft by Crossfire's powerful arm, gasped and wheezed, violently flailing about.

There was no fighting his way free. The other punks were speechless, unable to move in the moment.

"You filth!" Crossfire spat. "You think you're a match for me? That any of you are?"

Before anyone could respond, he brutally smashed the leader's head into the building wall to his left, crushing the punk's head as though it was an egg. The remaining three shrieked but remained motionless.

The sight of their slain leader laying in a bloody mess at their feet finally spurred Mohawk into action. Producing a flick-knife from his pocket, he charged at Crossfire.

"Gonna cut you, you bastard," Mohawk screeched.

Crossfire grabbed his assailant's arm, avoiding the knife, and with one, swift, deft movement, snapped his adversary's arm clean in two. Howling in pain and dropping to his knees, Crossfire lashed out with a savage kick, sending Mohawk careening into the same brick wall as his leader. Dead.

The remaining two punks had clearly had enough. The ferocity on display, the ease with which their compatriots had been dealt with, proved too much for them. They turned and ran as fast as their legs could take them.

Cowards, Crossfire thought, but he chose not to follow. His true purpose there lay elsewhere that night.

He looked up just as the rain began to fall. Quickly becoming a torrent, Crossfire rinsed his hands in a puddle before continuing on his journey.

His destination proved to be only a further two minutes' walk away. Reaching it, he checked the address against the address he had written on a slip of paper back at home base. They matched. It was a dingy Chinese restaurant but, perhaps not surprisingly considering it was acting as a front, the lights were on.

A bell above the door tinkled as he entered. There were no customers about. The place was squalid, the floor spotted with what appeared to be rodent feces, and bugs crawled about everywhere. It stank of everything but food.

At the counter at the far end, an elderly, overweight Chinese lady sat eating a bowl of noodles with chopsticks. She never raised her head as Crossfire approached her.

"Señor Lazar," he said. "I'm looking for Señor Lazar."

The lady briefly paused, raising her head slightly, before chowing down again without saying a word.

Behind her, a curtain parted, revealing a short, innocuous looking middle-aged man with short, frizzled gray hair.

"Señor Lazar?" Crossfire asked.

The man said nothing but beckoned Crossfire to follow.

Through the curtain, down a dimly lit narrow staircase, Crossfire soon found himself in a cavernous room. A high, domed ceiling rose above them, a shiny timber floor lay beneath. Counters and shelves littered with every form of weaponry and explosive imaginable, and some one couldn't even dream of, filled every corner of the room. For a man like Crossfire, it was an amazing sight to behold, akin to being a kid in a candy store.

"I recognized you immediately, of course," the man said in a Spanish accent. "It would be my proudest moment to make something for you."

"Señor Lazar?"

Lazar bowed in acknowledgment.

"I need weapons," Crossfire said, getting straight to the point. "Equipment. A protective suit. Pretty much the works. I have little money right now, but soon...I'll have an empire."

Lazar smiled, seemingly excited just to be in Crossfire's presence. "I can supply everything you need, and things you didn't think you needed. You can pay me when you are able. When the underworld knows I have equipped the great Crossfire, there will be plenty of business flowing my way." He smiled at that.

Lazar ambled over to a work-bench smothered in AK-47s and other such automatic arms even Crossfire couldn't identify. He opened a drawer and pulled from it a large unlined notepad. "Tell me specifically what you require, and I will start on the designs immediately."

* * * * * *

Harrison, Sloan, and Perez inspected Latham's ruined office. Charred furniture, shards of glass and other debris littered the once impressive room. Latham's famous busts were now little more than fragments and dust. It was a sight to behold.

"Get forensics in here now," Harrison ordered of a nearby constable as he led his two detectives out of the ruined office, down the stairs and into the lobby.

"They sure made a mess of the place," Sloan said, the memory of how the office looked still vivid in his mind. He lifted his cap and rubbed his head.

"Who, Sloan? Who?" Harrison barked. "I need to know who's responsible for this and we need to stop them now!"

"Could this be connected to the hit on Latham? The destruction of his home?" Perez said, rubbing her chin.

"I think that's a safe bet, don't you?" Sloan responded. "This is way too specific to be random terrorist attacks. Too grandiose to come from ISIL or Al-Qaeida or the like. I think we need to move forward with that assumption front and center in our minds."

"That gets us somewhere," Harrison said. "I think you're right. Until we hear from forensics, I need you both to check up on anyone who might have a grudge against Latham or any of his business dealings."

"That's a long list," Sloan said, raising his cap then instantly putting it back on. "Latham must have had thousands of enemies, all who would want him dead in a heartbeat. I don't see how that's gonna help us in any way. No, until we know more we need to shut this building down long term. Anything connected with Latham and his businesses must be locked down until we nail whoever's behind all this. That should limit any further attacks and loss of life."

"I don't think that's possible, but I'll see what I can do," Harrison said. "But the memorial is off limits."

"Memorial?" Sloan and Perez said in unison.

"The mayor wants to go all out with a massive public memorial for Latham, funeral parade in the streets, the works."

"That's insane!" Sloan cried. "The potential targets for this whack-job will be in the thousands. How are we supposed to protect them all out there in the open?"

"I agree, but my hands are tied. We all have our orders. If there *is* a further attack, you'll be there—we all will be there in force to take them down."

Sloan and Perez eyed each other, the former shaking his head with doubt. This had disaster written all over it. But Harrison was right about one thing. If there was to be a further attack at the upcoming memorial, he *would* be there. You could count on it.

"Commissioner Harrison?" another constable appeared before them.

"Yes, what is it?"

"A body has been discovered in the waterfront district. They say it's Charlie Grieco."

~ Chapter 6 ~

Paul, Leena, and Max convened in the Lair to discuss all that was currently known of the case.

"Two hits on Latham properties in two days, one larger than the other and one of which took out the man himself," Paul said. "Do we have any leads at all?"

"Without DNA samples to compare with, I can't tell for certain if the samples we have are the remains of Robert Latham or not," Max outlined. "But from what you tell me, as the servants had been sent home, I think we can safely assume they are."

"As you say," Leena chimed in. "One hit was larger than the other. Much larger. The first didn't just take out Latham himself or even his house but his entire estate. The second just ruined the man's office, by-and-large, and nobody else was killed."

"Right," Paul said. "So this was clearly a revenge motivated hit to kill Latham in the biggest most dramatic way possible. But it was more than that. I don't think the aim was just Latham himself, though, or his business. A message was clearly being sent."

"Why do you say that? And a message to whom?" Leena said.

"Because of the second hit. If the attacks were solely about Latham, then surely the one responsible would have leveled the Latham building, or at least done more damage than ultimately occurred. No, I don't think the second hit was actually about Latham or anyone associated with him at all."

Leena's face registered recognition of what Paul was driving at. "But...that can only mean...?"

"Yes," Paul said gravely as he started pacing. "I think they were after me. Not to kill me necessarily, but to send *me* a warning."

"Then..." Max started to utter.

"They know who I am, yes," Paul said. "This is an enemy we've met before. Who knows me—*us*—and knows my habits and has been, presumably, following me, keeping tabs on me. Possibly on all of us."

He continued pacing, rubbing his chin as he marched back and forth.

"But who could it be?" Max said. "We haven't one shred of evidence to suggest who it could be. We have several foes who know your identity."

"Most are dead, or presumed to be so," Paul said, ceasing his march and closely looking at Leena, noticing the concern etched on her beautiful face. "But only one of them was an expert in arms and assassination."

"It can't be him," Leena said after some thought. "You told me yourself you saw him die at Charlie Grieco's hands."

"I also saw him survive a point blank shot to the head only minutes earlier," Paul said. "We've all seen some amazing and frightening things in recent times. I have no proof, of course, but my gut tells me we're dealing with one of our deadliest adversaries." He turned to face the massive computer terminals to his side. "I don't know how it's possible...but I think Crossfire has returned!"

"So, what's our next step, Chief?" Max asked after a few moments.

"I need to see the place where that missile was launched. No doubt the police have gone through there with a fine-tooth comb, but I need to see for myself. They may have missed something." He turned to face them both. "The Wraith prowls again tonight."

* * * * * *

It was late afternoon before Sloan and Perez were finally able to reach the waterfront district. Exiting Sloan's bomb, he at once grimaced at the stink of the place. Not just of the sea, or a heavily polluted version thereof, but of decay. Rotting timber structures dotted the landscape. More modern, albeit abandoned warehouses, lay left and right, victims of the Global Financial Crisis. Garbage and goodness knew what else filled the gutters and numerous alleys.

"Where was the body located, Perez?" Sloan asked.

"A warehouse down on Bay Street, by the derelict docks there."

Plodding through the filthy streets for a couple of blocks, they reached a small warehouse with a few cop cars parked out front. Edging inside, the two detectives were met by a uniformed officer with a grim expression.

"Where's the stiff?" Sloan mumbled.

"Over this way," the officer indicated with a thumb.

The officer led the way through a maze of boxes and corridors. Rats scurried about their feet. "This warehouse is still in use to house imported canned food from Asia."

"Remind me to never again buy cheap food from the Dollar Store," Sloan said to Perez, who merely grinned in reply.

After a minute they came to a halt in a clearing which was illuminated by a large, shabby overhead skylight. There, at the far end up against the wall, was the body. Or what was left of it. Above it, written on the wall in what appeared to be blood were the words:

THE WRAITH IS NEXT!

Sloan lifted his cap, tried to hold his breath as best he could, for the body was beginning to putrefy. "Geez, what a mess."

"Who found the body?" Perez asked the officer.

"Caretaker," the cop replied. "He swears it wasn't here when he knocked off in the early hours of this morning."

"He's been dead longer than a few hours," Sloan said, crouching by the body. "The smell alone indicates that. And you can also see...there's very little blood on the floor in relation to the injuries. He was killed elsewhere."

"At least there's no doubt as to his identity," Perez said, crouching beside her partner. "The head and face are undamaged. This is definitely Charlie Grieco."

Sloan stood, scrunched his face. "He escaped from jail a month ago—leaving four guards dead—and was never seen or heard from again. Until now." He took a few steps back in an effort to escape the odor. "There was never any indication on who helped him to escape either."

"This murder has to be connected with the recent attacks, surely," Perez said, joining Sloan some feet away from the body. "There's no way this could be a coincidence."

"No way," Sloan agreed. "And whoever killed Grieco now has his sights set on our favorite caped crusader. That's gotta narrow the field of suspects down some."

"You realize how many punks in this city want The Wraith dead?" Perez asked.

"Sure, but how many with this sort of firepower, and this sort of skill?"

"I don't know," Perez admitted, "but it's a start."

"Are forensics on their way?" Sloan asked the officer after a few moments.

"We called it in, but they're stretched pretty thin with all that's happened the last couple days. I'm not sure when they're due to arrive."

Sloan snorted and punched his left palm in frustration. "Lock this place down. Don't let anyone else in here until the lab boys arrive. Got that?" He beckoned to Perez. "C'mon, let's get back to the office. I need to think. And to speak with Jim."

* * * * * *

The limousine came to a halt in the driveway of an impressively sized, though not huge, timber and brick home. The driver got out and opened the rear door, allowing Patrich Azufi to step forth. It was early evening but there were no lights on inside Azufi could see.

Where on Earth is she? he thought. *She didn't answer any of my calls from the hospital. The bimbo's probably out shopping again.*

He limped toward the front door, fumbled briefly with the keys, before finally making his way inside. The house was silent and dark, with no sight or sound of life anywhere.

Azufi switched the lights on and stood in the threshold wondering what to do next.

I should check in with the office, see how much damage there was.

He turned to his right, heading for his study adjacent to the deep brown timbered stairs.

"I'll get whoever tried to kill me," he murmured to himself. "I'll make them suffer for this."

"I wasn't trying to kill you," a voice emanated from the pitch black of the study. "I was sending someone a message."

"What the devil?!" Azufi said as he stormed into the room, switching the light on in the process. "Who the hell are you?!"

A stranger sat in Azufi's leather chair with a broad smile on his face, his hands pressed together beneath his chin.

"Wait a minute. I know you. I've seen your photo in the files back at the office."

"I'm flattered."

"Crossfire," Azufi whispered with some trepidation.

"You're going to help me," Crossfire said. "I have plans for you. For the entire organization."

"Why should *I* help *you*?" Azufi said bitterly. "You tried to kill me today. And...and..."

"Yes?" Crossfire said, still seated and still smiling.

"Oh my lord!" Azufi gasped. "You...*you* killed Latham. You took him and his wife out."

"Yes, I did," Crossfire readily admitted. "He had it coming, I can assure you. But you have no reason for complaint. I've advanced your career. In an instant you've become the new Boss of Bosses in this town." He stood. "Well, sort of."

"Wha...what do you mean?"

Crossfire approached Azufi, slapped him hard on his good shoulder. "I mean, good buddy, that you'll be this company's figurehead. Everyone will think you're the man in charge, but only you and I will know the truth—that I'll be running the show from now on."

"And if I refuse this ridiculous offer?" Azufi said. "All you can do is kill me, and if you kill me, you'll be the boss of nothing!"

Crossfire placed an arm over Azufi's good shoulder as if they were the best of pals. "Oh dear. Is it possible you haven't realized the position you're in?"

"Realized what?" Azufi said, managing to squirm away.

"Heard from your moll lately?" Crossfire laughed as the reality of Azufi's predicament hit home. "I can't honestly call her your wife seeing as you're not married, though you share the same surname already. She's a pretty little thing, though a little slutty for my liking. Still, she should prove something of a diversion for me as my vendetta continues." Crossfire circled Azufi as he spoke.

"You son of a—"

Crossfire grabbed Azufi's wounded arm and twisted. Azufi dropped to the floor, whimpering in pain like a baby. "Temper, temper. You need to work on that. Or grow some balls to back those words up."

"Don't...don't hurt her," Azufi begged, wheezing.

"Hurt her? Hurt little Niki? I wouldn't dream of it. Not if you co-operate and do *exactly* as I say."

Azufi dragged himself to his feet, stared at Crossfire through bleary eyes. "What do you want me to do?"

* * * * * *

METRO CITY CENTENNIAL PRISON – ONE MONTH EARLIER

The barred door swung closed behind him. He plopped down on the flimsy and grime-streaked bed and laid down.

"Charlie," he whispered to himself, "you're in a lotta pain in this place."

Grieco placed his hands behind his head on the pillow and sighed.

Damn Latham, he thought. *Damn The Wraith. I swear I'll get outta here one day. One day, they will both suffer. I will have my revenge.*

He then noticed an odd protrusion in his pillow. He sat up and reached into the pillow case, removing from it a small, folded handwritten note, which read:

JACK. 2AM. BE READY!

Grieco was perplexed by this, scrunching the note in his hands. He knew no one by that name, certainly not in prison, and what was he supposed to be ready for at 2AM? He wondered briefly if this was a setup, either by the corrupt staff, who he'd had run-ins with before, or from one of his fellow inmates. If the latter, one in particular came to mind— Flint Robbins.

Robbins was a brute of a man, and was the so-called King of Centennial Prison. No man within those walls would dare cross him. Robbins had also taken a disliking to Grieco the instant the latter had arrived there, and ever since then, he was constantly on guard, ever watchful for some sort of attack or malign plot against him. Thankfully, he wasn't completely without some influence within the prison fraternity, so he had managed to avoid any major issues thus far. But this note worried him.

Screw it. I'm not falling for this crap, Grieco thought. Still, he *was* concerned, there was no fighting it. *What if this crap comes for me here?*

After a few minutes consternation, he realized no matter what might occur, it was out of his hands. He hoped against hope the whole thing was simply a hoax, a joke to frighten him, to put him in his place, so to speak.

Yeah, that's it...a joke...

He lay back down, exhaustion clouding his thoughts. He'd had a busy, strenuous day. He still wasn't used to all the exertion—the manual labor—that came with being an inhabitant of such a place. He wasn't—

A metallic sound shocked him from his slumber. It was pitch dark. He must have been out for hours. He saw and heard nothing, and yet, he felt a presence there, someone close by.

"Is there anyone there?" Grieco said softly. No answer. "I know you're there. Whatever you're here to do, do it and get it over with."

As though in response, Grieco heard the cell door swing open and someone shuffled inside. The hair on the back of his neck bristled on end and sweat began to bead on his forehead.

"It's 2AM. Are you ready?" a man's voice came from somewhere in front of him.

"What the—?"

"Are you ready?" the voice repeated.

"Jack?" Grieco asked. "Are you Jack?"

The stranger grunted in the affirmative.

"What do you want? Who are you?"

There was an eerie silence for a few moments before Jack spoke again. "You want outta here, don't you?"

"I...I don't understand."

"I'm your way outta this dump," Jack hastily explained. "It's all been arranged."

Grieco's heart leapt for a moment at the mention of escape, a dream come true for him, but he then quickly thought it through. Had Latham regretted his decision to frame Grieco? Or was someone else in the organization eager for his return? Or another organization? His mind whirled with the myriad possibilities, none of which fully made any sense, and yet the man—Jack—was here all the same, seemingly to aid in his flight.

"Arranged by who?" Grieco finally asked.

"We don't have time for this," Jack said, flicking a small flashlight on, momentarily blinding Grieco in the process.

Rubbing his eyes, he managed to catch a slight glimpse of his apparent savior. It was no one he recognized, though he was wearing a guard's uniform.

"Okay, okay," Grieco muttered. "I'll trust you. I guess I have no choice. Lead the way out of this place."

In that moment, for some reason he couldn't quite fathom, he suddenly believed this was all legitimate. Doubts and fears of a setup now dissipated, though he honestly didn't know why. All he knew was he was willing to ride this feeling, this emotional high at the thought of impending freedom for all it was worth.

Jack swiftly retreated and bade Grieco to follow and to be quiet. Down the corridor leading to the mess hall, the only sound came from their footfalls and from the snoring of his fellow inmates as they passed their cells. They soon approached the gate which led through to the mess hall.

"Won't the guards see your light?" Grieco whispered. "There's no way outta here through there."

Jack turned, yanked Grieco sharply by the shirt collar. "Shut up!"

Stunned by the man's strength and effrontery, Grieco nonetheless did as he was told.

They continued on their way, down the lengthy corridor which, ultimately, led to the mess hall but first, a guard station. Grieco wondered how they would proceed and feared the worst.

Rounding a bend, Grieco was stunned by the sight that befell him. As they entered the guard station, one guard stood there, rigid and quiet, his mouth agape, but it was what surrounded the guard that shocked even Grieco. Three guards lay dead in voluminous pools of blood. Clearly this Jack was a serious force to be reckoned with.

"I did as you asked," the guard whimpered. "I opened all the gates you wanted."

"Very good," Jack replied, reaching to some sort of electronic mechanism strapped to the guard's torso and flicked a switch. "You won't be going kablooey anytime soon."

The guard visibly breathed a sigh of relief, but as soon as Jack turned away, he reached for a gun from a nearby counter. He needn't have bothered. Before anything, Jack whirled and flung a massive knife in little more than the blink of an eye. The blade buried itself in the guard's forehead, killing him instantly.

Grieco couldn't help himself and let out a wail of shock and fear. Jack lashed out with a right and—

Darkness.

Grieco awoke with a headache unlike any he'd experienced before. He battled to open his eyes. They wanted to stay shut. Wherever he was, the light was faint, but he couldn't see much anyway through his blurred eyes. He was obviously suffering from some sort of concussion.

He managed to rise from the tiny cot he found himself on and tried to steady himself. It wasn't easy.

"Where...where am I?" he found himself saying, trying to rub the sight back into his eyes.

"You're in my home, of sorts," a voice said.

"Jack? Is that you?"

"Yes," came the reply, "and no."

A substantial human form seemed to emerge from the mist in front of Grieco, who finally recognized him as he moved closer. Crossfire! This time clothed in a form-fitting black getup with a target logo at the apex of the chest.

"You," Grieco breathed. "You're back."

Crossfire grinned and took a little bow.

"You're Jack? You disguised yourself and broke me out? Why? What do you want from me?"

"We have a mutual enemy, you and I. You want Latham dead just as much as I do, I'm sure."

Grieco eyed Crossfire for a few moments. His mind raced with the memory of their last encounter. He remembered Crossfire seemingly perishing at his hand, but somehow he survived and escaped. Crossfire had proven to be an almost unstoppable foe. He didn't know how to feel, to react.

"Isn't that true?" Crossfire said.

"Yes, but..." Grieco started, not really knowing what to think or say.

"Right. So, you're going to help me end him once and for all," Crossfire said. "You know his access codes, his methods, security protocols, procedures."

"He would have changed many of those," Grieco blurted out.

"Some, no doubt, but not all," Crossfire said. "Despite that, you can assist me to allow me to slip in and out without causing a scene, like what happened in the jail tonight. I don't want Latham knowing I'd been there until the end. The *very* end."

Excitement was beginning to build within Grieco. This was his chance for revenge. There may never be another such opportunity, he thought. He had to take it.

"Do we have a deal?" Crossfire said, extending a hand.

Grieco waited a moment before he took it and shook. This was *his* moment. He could feel it, taste it. "Deal."

~ Chapter 7 ~

It was 3AM and a quick glance down confirmed the street below was deserted. The Wraith slid down his grapnel line at a steady pace as he searched for the window he wanted. While not as tall a structure as the Latham building it faced, Medway Plaza was nevertheless an impressive edifice. Fifty storeys of mainly offices and of modern construction, it was merely one of many such grand towers in Downtown Metro.

He stopped his descent as he approached the tarped-over opening. He looked across the street toward the Latham building. He could see the office had been the perfect vantage point for a missile attack. Parting the fabric, unhooking his grapnel from his belt and dropping dexterously inside, The Wraith tapped at his left temple, activating his night-vision lenses, which instantly dropped into place over the eye-holes of his cowl.

He scanned around the small office, but saw nothing untoward. Unfortunately, it had been cleaned and tidied already, the police obviously thinking they had gotten all they needed, or could, from the room and allowed the business's cleaning crew to come in and make the place as presentable as possible. Nevertheless, he continued his search for anything that might, just might, have been missed by both police and cleaner alike. After a few minutes of crouching and investigating every nook and cranny, he gave up.

It had been a forlorn hope from the start, he had to admit, he might find anything of value here, but with nothing other than a gut feeling to go on as to who was behind all this, he had to take a chance the police might have missed something. He hadn't thought the room would have been cleaned up quite so quickly, but that was the reality he now faced.

The Wraith straightened and activated his in-cowl radio. "Nothing to report here, the place is clean. Meet me at the agreed upon pick—"

An arrow whizzed by his head, missing it by inches, and slammed into the wall at the far end, embedding deeply into the plaster.

"Chief?" Max's voice rang out over the radio.

The Wraith logged off without a word and took cover behind the medium-sized—though solid—timber desk. He procured from his belt his mini-binoculars and peered through a crack in the tarp.

How could anyone have spotted me through this thing?

"You're probably wondering how I knew you were there, Wraith," a familiar voice rang out from behind.

The Wraith whirled but saw nothing. Nothing but the arrow stuck fast into the wall. Even from his current position, he could make out a widened bulge over the arrow's shaft.

A microphone, clearly, and there's a security camera on the wall above it. That's how he saw me.

"Peek-a-boo," the voice said.

A beeping sound, quickening its pace with every second, emanated from the arrow, and The Wraith knew he had to get out there and then. He leapt up and bounded for the tarp, diving through it and latching onto his line. As he pressed a button on the grapnel, an explosion tore through the office, tendrils of flame licking at his cape as he shot up toward the roof.

He landed with a thud but was quickly up on his haunches and searched the skyline once again with his binoculars. There, up on the Latham roof, someone appeared to be waving at him. He magnified the vision. No doubt about it—it was Crossfire, waving, a grin plastered on his face. No doubt seeing he'd been recognized, the villain sprinted for the far end of the roof. In moments he would be gone.

"Max!" The Wraith cried out over his radio. "Latham roof. Crossfire's there. He's on the move. Keep a watch for him. I'll meet you street-side in a moment."

Dashing toward the edge, The Wraith jumped into empty space, briefly careening downwards before grabbing onto the sides of his cape and allowing it to balloon outwards, acting as a parachute, slowing his descent. Achieving a perfect landing on the sidewalk, he raced over to the classic Daimler, which had just parked across the street in front of the Latham building.

"No sign of Crossfire around back or down this side of the building," Max said, pointing to the building's left. "Though he might have escaped before I got here."

"Or he might still be inside," The Wraith said, standing beside the car. "You should have seen him up there, beckoning to me. This is all just a game to him. He's playing with me. Toying with me."

"What do we do, Chief?"

"I have no choice but to play his game," The Wraith said. "Trap or not, this ends tonight."

He reached for his grapnel gun, aimed it skyward and fired. Once it had caught firm, he pressed a button and instantly raced for the heavens. In moments he had reached the roof.

There was no-one about. The Wraith swiftly followed the direction he'd seen Crossfire taking, reaching a doorway which led inside the building. It was open.

He definitely wants me to follow. He's expecting me.

He entered, noting all lighting, even the emergency illumination highlighting the exits, was switched off. He activated his night-vision lenses and cautiously proceeded down the stairs. He had no idea where his final destination lay, but he had no doubts Crossfire would somehow lead him there. He strained for any sight or sound of his quarry. If Crossfire had wished to escape, he'd had plenty of time to do so. Why was he eager for this encounter? Was it merely revenge, an attempt to trap him and do away with him? Possibly, but The Wraith thought it unlikely to be solely that. He felt sure there was something more.

Floor after floor he descended. Door after door he reached were closed and bolted. Crossfire had gone to a lot of trouble leading him somewhere specific. Did he have help from someone inside? That thought intrigued The Wraith as he continued his slow journey downwards.

Ultimately, having reached the thirty first floor, he came across an open door. He tentatively peered through. It was as dark as the rest of the building ostensibly was, though with his night-vision lenses in place, he could see the room opened up into a large gymnasium. All was still and quiet around him.

"You came," Crossfire's voice resonated from somewhere. "I knew you wouldn't fail to follow me."

"What do you want, Crossfire?" The Wraith called out in a commanding tone. "You've gotten your revenge. Latham and Grieco are dead at your hands."

"I see you appreciate my efforts already. Yes, those gangland scum are dead, and they deserved to die as you well know."

"Then I repeat—what do you want?"

Crossfire chuckled. "You think revenge upon them was my sole reason for returning from the dead? Could you truly be that naive?"

"If it's me you want, I'm here," The Wraith boomed. "Come out and face me. Let's end this here and now."

Powerful overhead lights strobed on, causing The Wraith to briefly flinch.

He's got control of the whole building? How? And how so quickly?

He immediately deactivated his lenses and allowed himself a few seconds for his vision to adjust. He then saw his enemy standing before him at the far end of the gym. Crossfire was as tall and powerful as before, but he was different this time as well, now wearing a skintight black outfit which appeared heavily armored in places at the same time. Some sort of weapon was attached to his right forearm, but it was hard to make out at this distance what it was. The room they stood in was massive and well-stocked with state of the art exercise equipment of every size and description, which The Wraith found somewhat ironic as he knew Latham detested physical exertion of any sort.

"This is hardly the end," Crossfire said. "No, no, nothing of the sort. This is only the beginning, Wraith. I'm going to make you suffer. Your interference in my plans last time cost me dearly. Now you're going to pay. When I'm through with you, you will beg me to end your life, and it will be up to me whether to grant you that mercy or not. I can't honestly say what I'll do...I haven't thought much beyond the torture I intend to inflict upon you."

The Wraith clenched his jaw. Crossfire looked fit and strong. He knew his nemesis's threats were worth taking seriously. Not only was Crossfire a formidable foe, but he also knew his true identity, knew his friends and loved ones. He had to end it now, lest all would be placed in serious danger. Then who would protect Metro City?

Without preemption, Crossfire discharged a projectile from his right arm. The Wraith easily side-stepped as it crashed into the wall behind him. In that instant, a cloud formed from the impact point; a thin mist wafted outward. The Wraith reached for the re-breather in his belt, but was unable to prevent himself taking a small breath of the gas now enveloping him.

Knockout gas!

Despite now inhaling pure oxygen from his re-breather, The Wraith suffered from his short dalliance with the gas. His legs buckled under him, though he managed to remain upright. It was that moment that Crossfire chose to strike.

Grunting like a man possessed, Crossfire charged, unleashing a series of powerful punches the Dread Avenger could only partially parry. With the effects of the gas not wearing off, Crossfire maintained the advantage. A left, a right, blows to the stomach, a knee to the face. Crossfire's assault was vicious and unrelenting. Even with his protective uniform shielding him from much of the power of Crossfire's fists, The Wraith nevertheless felt every impact.

"Ha! A bit of gas and you're done? This is the great Wraith, the Dread Avenger of the Underworld that has every hood in the city living in fear?" Crossfire kicked him in the gut, sending The Wraith to his knees. "You're nothing. *Nothing!*"

The Wraith wheezed, spat his re-breather out, tried to catch his breath quickly. Crossfire loomed, ready to strike again. The Wraith lashed out with a powerful uppercut to his opponent's jaw, causing Crossfire to stagger back.

"Oh ho, so there's a bit of fight left in you after all," Crossfire said, leering.

The villain moved in close to continue the battle, but The Wraith's Eyes of Judgment burst to electrical life, spewing forth with energies rarely seen in such intensity, the force of which caught Crossfire completely off guard, catching him fully in the midriff and sending him pummeling backwards, crashing into a nearby bench press.

"You will atone for your sins," The Wraith moaned. "Your evil ways have caught up with you. Now you will be cleansed...and know true judgment."

Crossfire sat up off the bench. He bled from his lip and appeared a little singed around the edges. He glared at The Wraith, fury and hatred burning in his eyes. "I told you this was only the beginning, Wraith. A sneak preview of what's to come."

He stood and threw something to the floor behind him. A thick, acrid smoke billowed. He took a step into it, allowing the cloud to wrap around him and, as it dissipated...he was gone.

"You're right," The Wraith said to himself in frustration. "This *is* only the beginning."

* * * * * *

Crossfire lurched into his warehouse bolthole. The light was low and it wasn't the cleanest place in town, even by Metro City standards, but he didn't care. All he needed was somewhere to lay low, to store his equipment, to occasionally rest and recuperate. And this place was as good as any.

He removed the intricate weaponry from his right arm, which Señor Lazar had designed and installed especially for him—a weapon that could fire bullets and arrows with equal deadliness and accuracy—and slammed it onto the table. He then plonked himself down on the adjacent cot and let himself relax for a moment.

As usual, while his body rested, his mind raced. Thoughts of his battle with The Wraith that night rambled through his brain. He hadn't had the fight all his own way, that was true, but he was now equally equipped and he felt he had the edge over his opponent, both physically and mentally. That notion brought him great joy and satisfaction. He was going to own this city, and no costumed freak—or anyone else—was going to stop him.

Sleep was beckoning, but then he thought of his prisoner in the next room. He needed to check on her.

"Niki," Crossfire said as he opened the sliding door and entered the dark, much smaller room which once served as the warehouse office. "Are you comfortable?"

Niki Azufi was incapable of answering, bound and gagged as she was, lying on another small, grimy cot. Her shoulder length brown hair was badly matted; she was voluptuous in body shape and was wearing nothing more than a negligee with a flimsy see-through robe over it. Her makeup was smeared from crying. She wasn't normally Crossfire's type, but then...he had to admit, even the slutty look appealed on occasion.

"I saw your beloved Patrich earlier. He's agreed to do as I say," he said as he sat on the edge of the cot beside her. "Which means you get to live. But I never said what condition you'd be in when I return you to him."

He leaned in close. Niki's face contorted in silent terror.

~ Chapter 8 ~

Max applied the last of the strapping around Paul's torso, who groaned slightly in the process. "There, that should do it."

"Thanks, Max."

Just as he stood and was about to put on a fresh shirt, Leena entered the Lair and, as Paul thought, appeared none too pleased to see her fiancé wounded.

"Paul," she cried. "Are you badly hurt?"

"I'm fine," Paul said, though turning to face Leena caused him to grimace a little. "Max has patched me up so I'm as good as new."

"What happened, was it..."

"Crossfire? Oh yes. My gut instinct was proven correct. He's returned, and he's responsible for everything—Latham and Grieco's murders, the attacks—everything."

"What does he want?" Leena asked. "Revenge against Latham? Against you?"

"All of the above," Paul said as he tried to stretch the kinks out of his muscles. He didn't think any ribs were broken, but he was very sore all the same. "It's more than that, though. Something else is driving him. His plans are bigger than simple revenge, I know it. We just have to find out what those plans are and stop him."

"Come on, darling," Leena said, giving Paul a kiss and placing a gentle arm over his shoulders. "Let's get some breakfast upstairs."

A few minutes later, they sat at the compact nook within the kitchen, eschewing the rarely-used formal dining room, and took a sip from the excellent coffee placed before them by their butler, Jonathan Simpson.

"Breakfast will now be served," Simpson announced.

Paul smiled and nodded his thanks.

"So," Leena started, resting her chin in her hands, "what is Crossfire after if not revenge?"

"Revenge is part of this, no doubt. A *big* part. But he has something else in train. I just wish I knew what."

Leena looked at him with care.

"He's more powerful, more resourceful than ever, Leena. And better equipped. He's prepared for me, no question. Probably been planning his assault on the city for months."

Leena weakly smiled, but said nothing for some moments before speaking. "Well, you better eat up." Simpson laid his breakfast of two boiled eggs and toast down on the table. "It's going to be a big day. Latham's funeral is today and the mayor has decided to make a real show of it."

"What do you mean?" Paul said.

"The morning paper, sir," Simpson said, laying the broadsheet *Metro City Times* on the table, as well as Leena's breakfast of bran muffins. The headline said it all. Paul was not amused.

"The fool!" he muttered. "Crossfire could have a field day with this. I think I'll alert Sloan as to just who we're dealing with here."

"And you've been invited as one of the VIPs. But do you think he would target just anybody?" Leena asked. "Even innocent bystanders?"

Paul clenched his jaw. "If that helped further his plans, I don't think he would hesitate to kill anyone that stood in his path, or cause any kind of carnage. The size and scope—the ferocity—of his attacks so far show he wants to spread fear and terror throughout the city. And we have to be ready to do whatever it takes to stop him."

He looked at Leena, saw the deep concern etched in her beautiful features. He didn't want to alarm her any more than he had to, but they needed to be strong and resolute, and prepared for anything. Crossfire was *capable* of anything, and the city depended on them for salvation.

* * * * * *

Sloan carefully eyed Perez as she sat at her desk in front of his. He had to admit, she did look a little improved of late, but wondered if that was because of their heavy involvement in the Latham/Grieco case taking her mind away from that...other matter. Perez had recently been suffering, as had much of the city, with a strange sort of depression, a mysterious melancholy that had descended upon the city, washed over it like a tsunami and had never receded. Even Sloan himself had felt the effects of it until he realized...

"What?" Perez said in a huff, as though she had eyes on the top of her head.

"Are you kidding me?" Sloan said in mock shock.

"You've been staring at me for the last few minutes. Is there something wrong with my clothes? Something in my hair?"

"I was just wondering," Sloan said softly, leaning forward, "how you were feeling? Any better? I know you were—"

"I'm fine, Bob. Truly I am. And I'd rather not talk about it if it's all the same with you."

Sloan held his hands aloft in acquiescence, but he knew better. Perez's mood hadn't changed at all. She had just gotten better at hiding it.

"Sloan! Perez!" Commissioner Harrison bellowed. "You both better be getting ready."

"I can't believe we're being forced to take part in this farce," Sloan grumbled. "We're running a murder investigation here not crowd control."

"I need every available officer on the streets for this parade," Harrison said, "especially those I can trust. So get to it. You two should be downtown already."

"We're on it, sir," Perez said, grabbing her partner by the arm and dragging him from his desk. "We'll be there soon."

"I can't believe this," Sloan said, still grumbling as he drove them both toward their downtown destination. "What are we supposed to do, babysit Latham's corpse?"

"There was no body, remember?" Perez said. "This is a symbolic burial only."

"Symbolic? Symbolic my ass! The man was scum personified, and we're supposed to salute him as some sort of hero? Give me a break."

"The mayor wanted to show the city—"

"The mayor?" Sloan said in indignation. "Mayor Hutchison is a turd. He was so far up Latham's ass he'll never be able to clean the stench off himself. I don't know what the mayor's thinking now, but this has to be some sort of thank you for Latham funding his last electoral campaign."

"I don't know..." was all Perez said in reply to Sloan's tirade.

They came to a halt at the end of Main Street, the impressive Victorian Era City Hall facing them. Sloan slammed his door closed in disgust as he exited. His cell phone then beeped an incoming message. He pulled it unceremoniously from his pants pocket and looked at its screen.

Crossfire is the one responsible for the murders and attacks. You can contact me via this number—it is untraceable —and I will contact you when needed. Stay alert - W

"What the...?" Sloan uttered.

"Bob? Something wrong?"

Sloan caught himself, realized his mistake. "Oh, nothing, nothing. Just Janet annoying me," he said in reference to his wife.

W...that's The Wraith obviously, Sloan thought. *So, we're on close speaking terms now. Good. Crossfire back from the dead? No explanation how or when, but it tallies with the scene where we found Grieco's body...and I trust The Wraith knows what he's talking about.*

"Earth to Sloan," Perez piped up. "You're zoning on me."

"What?"

"That must have been some text from Janet."

Sloan frowned at her but said nothing. He inched forward, flashed his badge, and joined a flotilla of uniformed police officers milling about all the activity. A giant stage had been erected just ahead, with national, state and city flags surrounding it. A podium, with the mayor's seal gracing its front, sat proudly atop the stage.

"So, this is where the show will start?" Sloan asked the nearest uniformed cop, a tall, slim man in his mid-thirties most likely.

"Yes, sir," the cop replied. "The mayor will deliver his keynote speech at 10AM, with other dignitaries and VIPs seated either side of him. The coffin will then emerge from City Hall, which the dignitaries and VIPs will then carry down Main Street until they reach the hearse way down there." He pointed far down the lengthy boulevard. "Where it will then be taken to Brookwood for burial."

Sloan rolled his eyes at all that. All this rigmarole for a man so corrupt, so heinous, just galled the heck out of him. How much taxpayer money was being wasted on this rubbish Heaven only knew.

"How long is all this expected to take?" Sloan asked.

"Who knows," the cop said. "We've been told to expect thousands of mourners lining the streets, so it could go on for hours."

"Great," Sloan said, shrugging his shoulders. "So we have to babysit a stiff all day."

Perez was about to speak up but Sloan stopped her cold. "I know, I know. There's no body. This is a symbolic burial only." He turned to face the cop once again. "Okay, take me through your security procedures in place here. We're going to have to make some changes."

* * * * * *

Paul strode into his ample walk-in closet and was instantly surrounded on three sides with his extensive collection of bespoke suits and shirts created by his tailor Jon DeBoise at

Cad & the Dandy in London, and handmade English shoes from Gaziano & Girling. In the center of the expanse was a long, slender deeply timbered buffet, with drawers opening on either side, crescending into a comfortable leather seat at the far end.

He opened the top drawer on the right, and out slid an impressive series of watch winders featuring a varied selection of fine timepieces from Rolex, Omega, Jaegre Le Coutré and many others. However, he reached for his current favorite, his Tudor Heritage Black Bay Blue and put it on. He next chose a black shirt, burgundy tie and charcoal-peaked lapel single-breasted suit and simple black derby shoes to complete the look. Invited to take part in the grand affair of Robert Latham's funeral procession, he wanted to look the part. He was supposed to be in mourning, after all.

"Darling, you're running late," Leena said, popping her head around the corner. "You sure you don't want me there with you?"

"I'll be fine," Paul said as he completed the four-in-hand knot in his tie. "It's bad enough one of us has to attend this sham. I know you're going to be busy today, what with the opening of the new branch library. Sloan now knows what we're all dealing with, so he should have made better provisions in case of another attack. But, sham or not, I need to be there."

He smiled, gave her a quick kiss, and was off.

In twenty minutes he had reached the site of the memorial service and parked his Rolls. There were already masses of people lining the street up ahead, and it was only going to build up from there.

In moments he had entered City Hall and strode through the marvelously intricate sandstone lobby toward the function room, where all those invited were due to congregate prior to the commencement of the service.

Commissioner Harrison greeted him the moment he entered. "Paul, good to see you again so soon."

"I'm honored to be invited. Such a sad occasion, too. I doubt the city will soon recover from such a great loss."

"Metro City is stronger than you give her credit," Harrison declared.

"Some fine words there," a man said as he approached them. Paul recognized him as Mayor Hutchison, a short, rubicund man of thinning locks, though they had never before met. "Happy to meet you, Mr. Sanderson? I've heard a lot about you, of course."

"Paul, this is our new mayor, John Hutchison," Harrison said.

The two shook hands.

"Such a tragedy," Paul said, laying it on thick. "And I read that Charlie Grieco has also been killed recently. So much death and misery." He shook his head as he spoke.

"Yes, we're looking into that as well," Harrison stated. "No stone will be left unturned, I can tell you that."

"Good to hear, Harrison," Hutchison said. "We need to get these maniacs off our streets. Robert Latham was one of our most stellar citizens, a baron of industry and philanthropist of wide renown. He was also my friend. I expect you to find who was responsible for this outrage and have them put away."

Harrison weakly smiled and nodded in agreement.

"Mr. Mayor?" a well-dressed young man cried out from the doorway. "The governor has just called...he won't be able to make it today."

"Damn! He sure left it late to send his apologies," Hutchison said, clearly perturbed. "Well?"

"Uhh...it's time to start the service," the young man said. "You're running substantially behind schedule."

"Fine, fine," Hutchison said, looking down at his wristwatch with some irritation. "We'll be out shortly. Well, gentleman, shall we head out?"

They filed out of the function room and City Hall itself in two-by-two formation. Paul took a seat on the stage at the far right of the center podium alongside a somewhat downcast-looking Patrich Azufi. Harrison sat on the other side of Azufi, who was then followed by Governor Rogerson's empty chair. To the left of the podium sat the Deputy Mayor and two other prominent city businessmen.

Paul glanced up and out toward the massive crowd seated and standing before them. Behind them, thronging both sides of Main Street as far as the eye could see, and barricaded from the center of the street itself, were possibly thousands of people who had come to pay their respects. Robert Latham had employed many people in the city, and had contributed to many restoration and beautification projects in Metro, as well as many charities across a wide spectrum of causes, so perhaps the mass outpouring of grief was only natural to those that did not really know the man behind the facade.

"Ladies and gentlemen," Hutchison announced over the microphone, "thank you for coming here today to salute and say farewell to a truly great man. Robert Latham meant much to me personally and to you all. I was fortunate to be able to call him my friend. Now, Commissioner Harrison here has guaranteed me this very hour that whomever was responsible for this vicious murder, and the attacks on our fair city, will be apprehended as soon as possible, and I know he is a man of his word. We will not tolerate such acts of wanton violence in Metro any longer, and I can assure you this will not happen again."

Paul looked around for any signs of Crossfire, but it was impossible to see anything specific in a crowd of such size. He was able to make out a large police presence, both on the ground and on the surrounding rooftops, but with what the city had gone through recently, he felt that only natural. If Crossfire was in amongst the milling crowd, it would be impossible to tell.

"Robert Latham," Hutchison continued, "was a very special man. Born into poverty, he started with nothing, got a job in the mail room of Cratchit & Marley Accountants, worked his way through college and, eventually, climbed the corporate ladder, taking the business over many years later upon the deaths of both Cratchit & Marley, turning it into the global conglomerate it is today. With interests ranging from electronics to fossil fuels to construction and a whole lot more, Latham Industries now employs many thousands of people, here in Metro City and throughout these United States and, indeed, around the world."

Boy, Paul thought, *he's really going on about the man. No signs of Crossfire at least. With all these people about, I hope he stays away.*

"I want you all to know that your jobs are secure. I've spoken with the new head of Latham Industries, Mr. Patrich Azufi here," Hutchison said, gesturing to Azufi, who smiled wanly in return, "and he has assured me it's business as usual for the foreseeable future."

The masses erupted into applause at that, their sheer exultation palpable. Hutchison sure knew how to play to the crowd, Paul thought. He wasn't a politician on the up for nothing. Paul wondered just how far Hutchison's ambitions lay.

"Now, without further ado," Hutchison said, a crack in his throat, "we will commence the funeral procession. God bless you, Robert Latham, God bless Metro City and God bless these United States of America." The mayor paused for effect, lapping up the cheers, then turned to face those seated either side of him. "Gentlemen."

A Scottish funeral dirge began to play over the loudspeakers as the mayor led the way across the stage and down it. Uniformed police officers emerged from City Hall carrying a large ornate gilt coffin. Descending the hall stairs, they carefully placed the coffin on the ground, then formed an honor guard around it. Hutchison, Paul and the others then took their place either side of it, lifted it and placed it on their shoulders. The uniformed officers then led the way slowly, inexorably down Main Street.

If Crossfire wanted to strike, Paul thought, *this would be the moment.*

With the dirge playing on a loop in the background, the group gradually marched with their cargo past the multitudes of people. Paul noticed that many of them were weeping, legitimately grieving for the man, whom Paul knew to be one of the most evil he'd ever encountered.

Within some minutes, they'd traversed the length of Main Street and reached the waiting hearse. The rear of the vehicle opened and the group carefully placed the coffin within. As Paul closed the door, shots suddenly rang out. Dozens in the crowd began to scream, causing others to start to rumble. Paul knew panic would soon reign.

Oh no. This is just what I feared.

The sound of engines revving began to build as the crowd started to riot, crashing through the barricades and overwhelming the cops. The police were no match for that amount of people.

Paul scanned the rooftops and windows for any sign of a shooter, but couldn't see anything untoward. He tried to move forward, make his way back toward City Hall, but it was almost impossible to fight his way through the masses.

At that moment, the roar of approaching motorcycles drowned out all else. Paul was forced to leap to safety as a bevvy of leather-clad bikers stormed past him.

"What the hell is going on here?" Harrison shouted above the din a short distance away.

An army of bikers certainly wasn't Crossfire's style, Paul felt sure, but then again...

There, up ahead. It's him!

A tall man wearing a hoodie and sweats a short distance ahead looked up and their eyes met, locking briefly together.

It was Crossfire!

The villain didn't waste a moment, turning to run, barging through the crowds, violently pushing those in his way to one side in a desperate attempt at escape. Paul didn't dare tarry and made to follow. He wasn't about to let Crossfire escape a second time.

The bikers, at least ten of them Paul estimated, began circling and firing with automatic weaponry at police officer and citizen alike. They clearly didn't care who was caught up in the melee. Paul ducked and weaved as he sprinted, spotting Sloan on the sidelines feverishly directing the police response to the threat.

Up ahead, he saw Crossfire run smack bang into a biker, who held an automatic rifle aloft. Paul could now identify him as a member of the Bandidos gang, a new menace to Metro City that had recently attempted securing a beachhead in town to run their drugs and protection rackets. No doubt they thought to capitalize on Latham's death to try and move in on the departed crime lord's territory.

The biker smiled, but was too complacent, no doubt thinking he had the edge. Crossfire clearly felt differently, yanking the gun from the biker's hands, causing the biker to tip forward and off the cycle completely. Without hesitation, Crossfire leapt aboard the prone Harley, spun it round on its wheels and shot away.

Not again.

Paul looked behind him, saw Sloan and his fellow cops taking control of the situation, and ran as fast as he could for his Rolls. Another few moments and he reached his vehicle, gunning its V12 engine to life and roared after his arch foe.

Crossfire had a substantial lead but, thankfully, the streets for a certain radius around Main were relatively clear, and Paul was able to put his powerful car to good use, gaining ground on the fugitive in a short space of time.

He saw Crossfire turn, seeming to notice how close Paul was, then turned sharply again, aiming the Harley into a narrow, trash-strewn alley. Paul followed suit, guiding the Rolls perfectly through the muck.

Crossfire continued to try and shake his pursuer, wildly careening through the streets and by-lanes of Metro, but Paul stuck to his rear no matter what. Crossfire then lurched his cycle up onto the sidewalk, pedestrians fleeing and jumping for their lives. Paul pressed on his horn in an attempt to warn those ahead of the danger they faced. Did Crossfire have any specific destination in mind, Paul wondered, in an effort to trap him, or was he merely madly trying to get away, anywhere.

Crossfire then screeched into Freedom Plaza, catapulting down the lengthy flight of stairs at remarkable speed. Paul had no choice but to follow, the Rolls bumping noisily downwards. Crowds of people out enjoying the fine weather ran in a panic in all directions, all trying to avoid the speeding death coming their way.

Back into the streets, Paul guided the Rolls alongside Crossfire, who turned to face him, fury etched into his features, before he sped forward. Crossfire, having regained the lead, then did the unthinkable: he pointed his motorcycle into a shopping mall parking lot. Avoiding families with their shopping carts, the villain pummeled through the glass front doors, sending deadly shards of glass everywhere, with Paul still close at his heels, blaring the car horn once again.

Is he mad? He can't escape me here.

Men, women and children flailed about, but as far as Paul could tell, none were impacted by either of their vehicles. Past candy stores, boutiques, jewelry stores, pop-up and concession stands, they raced until they reached the other end of the mall. Crossfire crashed through the rear exit, causing further mayhem at every opportunity.

This has gone on far enough. I have to end this now!

Paul slammed his foot on the gas and was soon speeding alongside his quarry once again. Before another moment was lost, he pressed a button beside the handbrake. A missile shot out of the Rolls' left front wheel, exploding into the front of the Harley. The cycle crashed sideways, Crossfire spewing forth over the handle bars, sliding across the asphalt before slamming into a large dumpster by the mouth of an alleyway.

Paul brought the Rolls to a stop, quickly got out, and reconnoitered the scene. Thankfully, they had by then reached a more rundown section of the city and it was largely deserted, save for a few winos and bums.

The sound of approaching police cars sounded. Paul knew he had to act quickly. He moved over to where Crossfire lay.

The villain was gone.

It had only been a moment, but in that short space of time, Crossfire had apparently vanished. Paul spun on his heels, looking this way and that, straining for any sign of his foe. There was none. The police were nearing fast. He couldn't let the cops find him there. There were too many questions he'd have to answer. Too many he'd be *unable* to answer. Despite desperately wanting to continue the hunt, he knew he had to get out of there, fast.

What's that?

There, under the dumpster, he spotted a manhole cover, and it appeared to be slightly ajar.

The police were nearly there. Swiftly, he jumped back into his Rolls and sped away. With dusk looming, he vowed to return as soon as night fell.

~ Chapter 9 ~

Gurneys filled with the wounded and the dead were being wheeled away as Sloan and Perez watched on with heavy hearts. Despite all their precautions, they had been unable to prevent a tragedy, though Sloan felt sure it could have been worse had his procedures not been put into place.

"Sloan," a disheveled Commissioner Harrison said. "Report."

"Three dead, dozens injured."

"Damn," Harrison said under his breath.

"This should have been avoided, Commissioner," Sloan said. "You know that as well as I do. This moronic parade should never have gone ahead under the current circumstances."

"Excuse me, Detective?" Mayor Hutchison said, appearing from the sidelines, also looking somewhat disheveled.

"You heard me," Sloan said with some acidity.

"This memorial service was an important—"

"Cut the crap!" Sloan spat. "This service should never have gone ahead while the threat was as yet unidentified or apprehended." Though Sloan now knew whom The Wraith thought responsible for everything, and he only received that information immediately prior to the service. "No matter what precautions we took, in such a short space of time and with the amount of civilians crammed into a relatively small area, we were sitting ducks for some sort of an attack."

"But...but..." Hutchison sputtered, but Harrison held up a hand, silencing him.

"Can we be sure this attack can be linked with the previous ones?" Harrison asked.

"I don't think it is," Sloan said and Perez nodded her agreement beside him. "This looks like the work of the Bandidos gang flexing their muscles. Unless, of course, they're working with, or for, whoever's behind all this."

"Not likely," Harrison said, "knowing how those biker gangs operate."

"So," Perez said, "what we have here is one of life's horrible little coincidences."

"I think so," Sloan said.

"Okay, then we need to set up a task force to combat these bikers. Sloan, Perez, take some men and point their investigations in that direction. I want the both of you to continue solely on the previous attacks and, if the two investigations coalesce, liaise together accordingly."

"Done," Sloan said, thinking the idea a good one.

"I'll direct things on the ground here for the present," Harrison said. "I think that's for the best, don't you, Mr. Mayor?"

Hutchison looked nonplussed, merely nodding in silent reply.

"We better get to it, Bob," Perez said, leading the way over to Sloan's battered sedan.

They marched slowly, watching their steps through the detritus that had only recently been a celebration of a man's life. Banners and flags lay in tatters on the street while a sizable chunk of the stage had been blasted to smithereens by automatic rifle fire. And groups of men and women with minor injuries were still being attended to by ambulance officers. Sloan sighed. So much horror, and these past few days were only a small slice of what Metro had gone through the past few years. Would it ever end? Whatever the answer to that was, he'd had a gutful of it. All of it. But he had a job to do and he wasn't about to let his fellow officers down.

Or Metro City.

* * * * * *

Patrich Azufi slid into his chair in his old, much smaller and windowless office at work, and bent forward over the desk, placing his head into his hands. He felt like weeping. What a mess his life had become. Even just a week ago he had been on the up and up. He was about to be promoted by the King of Metro into a leading position within the organization...as soon as he bopped off his predecessor, which he had promptly done. And he was living with the woman he desired. Sure, he had left his wife for her, but what did he care? He wasn't after commitment, after all. He was after action. Action at work, action at play. He was going to be a big man. But now...now...

The office door banged open, with Crossfire limping inside.

"What the hell?" Azufi shrieked.

"That damn Wraith and his toys," Crossfire lamented, flopping down onto the small love-seat beside the door. "He nearly had me. I only just managed to get away. If it wasn't for the cops—"

"What are you babbling about?" Azufi said, standing. "And what do you think you were doing at the memorial service today? How could that stupidity profit you in any way? I could have been killed!"

"Shut up!" Crossfire barked. "I wasn't responsible for today's shambles. I was just there to...to..."

"Then...why? Who?"

"It was some biker gang," Crossfire said, partially ignoring Azufi. "Have you heard of the Bandidos?"

"They...they've been causing us a little trouble of late," Azufi said. "Establishing some new drug rings, starting to launder money, other small stuff. Mr. Latham said—"

"They've clearly decided to take over as of today," Crossfire pointed out. "They've just declared war. And I'm happy to give them one."

"Wha...what do you mean?"

"Set the entire organization onto them," Crossfire said. "We're going to wipe them out."

"You're going to start a gang war? Now?" Azufi said with some shock.

"No, I'm going to end one," Crossfire said, standing. He lurched forward. "But first, I want you to contact the chief of the local water company. Call in some favors."

"The what? Good lord, why?"

"The sewers are awfully backed up, wouldn't you say? Especially this time of year. I think they could do with a good cleaning. Let's get them flushed out. Get on the phone. Whatever it takes, make it happen!"

* * * * * *

The Wraith dropped down into the sewers with a lithe grace and activated his night-vision lenses. He knew it was now too late to immediately capture Crossfire, but if perhaps he could somehow find a clue as to the villain's whereabouts, maybe all was not yet lost.

The fetid water was ankle deep and rats scurried about in all directions, but The Wraith remained resolute in his search for any trace of Crossfire's flight. It would be almost impossible to uncover anything of worth amongst the feculent muck, but he had to try.

"Chief, any luck?" Max's voice came over the radio.

"Not yet," The Wraith replied. "Stay in position. I don't know how long this will take."

The Wraith searched and probed the long dark tunnel as best he could. Ultimately, the narrow passage opened up high atop a much wider expanse, a series of further channels branching off into several directions far below. There was no telling which, if any, Crossfire might have taken. This had proven to be the dead end he had feared. There was no other option but to head back.

He trudged back the way he had come, intending to reach his entry point into this subterranean world and then proceed further beyond it. It was conceivable he might find something of value there.

Continuing on, the water receded a little but the disgusting accumulation of filth increased. Now along with the feces there were diapers, wet wipes, tampons and fatty, oily deposits lining the tunnel walls like the clogged arteries of a person requiring heart bypass surgery. The repellent stink caused him to retch slightly.

"Nothing in this section of the tunnel either," The Wraith reported via radio. "Though it would be nigh on impossible to see even if there was something here." He coughed. The pong was becoming unbearable. "What was that?"

The distant sound of running water had quickly evolved into that of a raging torrent.

"Chief?" Max said.

Terror began to build within The Wraith as he realized his situation. There, up ahead, he could see a wall of water barreling toward him. He had only seconds to act, pulling his re-breather from his belt and placing it into his mouth. He braced for impact as best he could, but there was no resisting the tsunami that smashed into him.

"CHIEF?!"

There was nothing he could do to fight the immense surge of water. He was pummeled from his feet, sent crashing back, unable to stop himself from being swept away by the incredible current. He desperately clawed around himself, trying for any handhold possible, but amongst the slippery muck, there was no hope. The chasm at the far end of the tunnel behind him was his destination. And perhaps his doom.

Moments lengthened but nothing could stop him from careening out of control. Then, by some stroke of fortune, he latched onto something with his left hand and held on with all his might. The maneuver almost wrenched his arm out of its socket, causing him to grunt in agony, but he held firm. His re-breather failing him—it was only made to last a few minutes maximum—he struggled to raise his head above the water level. As he did so, he spat it from his mouth and took a deep breath. Stench or no, his lungs were burning for lack of air.

It was then he realized he had latched onto the steel ladder leading up to the manhole by which he had first entered the sewers. Heaving a sigh of relief, he climbed the ladder in some pain, crawled through the manhole and out from under the dumpster, then lay there in a heap, sucking in the sweet, fresh air by comparison.

"Max," he called out via his radio. "Come." His mind then whirled into unconsciousness.

When he opened his eyes he found himself comfortably resting in his bed at home, his beloved Leena sitting beside him, watching over him. The bright sunshine streamed through the arched windows in thin slivers.

"Thank goodness you're awake," she said, leaning down to kiss him.

"How long have I been out?" Paul said in a hoarse whisper.

"A while. It's nearly eleven. I let work know I'd be a little late coming in today."

Paul sat up, groaned a little.

"Paul, be careful. You hurt your shoulder again, the one you damaged while battling the Cobra."

He flexed his left shoulder. A little stiff and painful, but nothing he couldn't handle. "I'm fine. It'll heal. It always does."

By Leena's expression Paul could tell she wasn't so sure. He smiled at her to try and reassure her. "You better get off to work. I'll be fine, trust me."

Leena stood. "What on Earth happened down there last night?"

"I fell off my surfboard," Paul tried to joke. Leena did not look amused. "I'm fine, really. It was just a bit of water."

Leena placed her hands on her hips. "A bit of water? From what Max told me he heard, it sounded like a tidal wave hit you. How could that have happened?"

Paul stood, stretched his entire body. Yes, his shoulder still hurt but he would never let on to Leena just how much. "However it happened is immaterial. The end result is the same: Crossfire has escaped me again."

Leena gazed into his eyes, clearly deeply concerned. She kissed him again and checked her Rolex watch. "You're right, I better get going. But I want you to promise me to take it easy today. You were badly hurt last night and I want you to give yourself a chance to recuperate. Even with your amazing healing abilities, you need to rest a little."

"Yes, ma'am."

Once Leena had gone, he reached up to his left shoulder and squeezed it. It still hurt like hell. While he hadn't been able to hide his discomfort from Leena completely, he wasn't about to admit to her how much pain he was really feeling. Yes, it would heal, and quickly, but right now it was excruciating.

"Oh, you're up," Max said while passing the bedroom door. He poked his head in. "How are you feeling?"

"A little stiff to say the least," Paul said. Max raised an eyebrow. "Okay, this shoulder bloody hurts." He tried rotating his arm. It was extremely painful, but at least there was the full range of movement. "I assume you cleaned me up last night?"

"Oh sure," Max said. "Fully disinfected and deloused in the Lair." Max grinned broadly.

Paul weakly smiled but couldn't muster much good cheer. "He's been one step ahead of me at every turn, Max. We're still no closer to finding Crossfire let alone apprehending him. He's covered his tracks well."

"Then we need to try and anticipate him," Max said. "Discern what his plans are. If we can do that, then we'll get him."

"Crossfire's plans," Paul ruminated, as much to himself as to Max. "Let's start with revenge. He wants to revenge himself against me for thwarting his scheme the last time we met. Revenge against Robert Latham for betraying him and his team in Iraq, and against Charlie Grieco for all of the above."

"Right."

"He's achieved his aim against two of them. Only I remain."

"You said before you thought there was more to Crossfire's plans than just revenge," Max pointed out.

"He's trying to play games with me," Paul said. "He told me he intends to torture me before finally killing me. But..."

"But?"

"What was he doing at the Latham memorial service? He wasn't there to cause any trouble. He was unarmed, in sweats."

"So you don't think he organized the attack at the funeral? He's *not* working with the Bandidos?" Max asked.

"No, I don't think so. Not his style," Paul said, pacing, rubbing his jaw in deep thought. "The question then remains —What was Crossfire doing there?"

"Maybe he *was* planning something and was simply put off by the biker gang?" Max said, then shook his head. "No, wait, you said he was unarmed. Hmm..."

"I think," Paul said after some further consideration, "he just wanted to be there, to revel in the glory of attending the funeral of the man he hated, the man he had murdered. In the same way serial killers often relive their crimes, revisit the scenes of their crimes, to repeat the thrill of their actions."

"Okay," Max said, taking this theory in, "if that's the case, how does this knowledge get us any closer to stopping Crossfire?"

"It doesn't," Paul said with some consternation, "but it gives us some insight into his state of mind. Think about it. It was a mistake attending that funeral, especially unarmed. The sort of mistake Crossfire wouldn't normally make. So, his plans for revenge for...whatever have somewhat unhinged him. He's starting to make errors of judgment. We can surely use that to our advantage."

"It's a plan, of a sort," Max said, though he looked at Paul with a questioning glance. "But you're not convinced."

"It means the next move is Crossfire's. And that worries me. It worries me a lot."

~ Chapter 10 ~

A group of leather-clad bikers sat alongside each other in the bar of their clubhouse, all six of them swigging down large glasses of beer. The odor of ale and cheap liquor permeated everything around them. The barman, himself a sturdy, broad-chested biker-type, knowingly smiled at them.

"You guys are crazy," the barman said. "You ran straight into a bunch of cops all guns blazing. You're nuts."

"We got our message across," the gang leader, Marcus, an immense behemoth of a man with a shock of long red hair cascading down his back, said. "We showed this city who's taking over now that Latham's dead and buried. And the cops could barely touch us."

"What a rush," said the biker at the far end of the bar to Marcus's left, somewhat the worse for drink. "I capped off at least five."

"I told you we'd be set," Marcus said, taking another gulp from his stein. "With Latham gone, this city is ours for the taking. There's a goldmine here just waiting for us to tap its riches. Drugs, arms, you name it, we can do it."

Another swallow and he slammed the empty glass upon the bar, then indicated to the barman to fill it back up again. Before that could be done, a deep rumbling like an earthquake filled their ears, followed by a shattering of glass and mortar.

"What the—" Marcus started.

Other gang members streamed into the bar area. One screamed, "It's a raid!" Another, "They've sent the army after us!"

Marcus was quick to act. "Behind the bar, all of you," he said. "Grab the weapons there. Wait for my signal before firing."

The sounds of automatic gunfire echoed throughout the building instantly followed by the death cries of their comrades. It sounded to Marcus like World War III was raging just a few feet from them. Abruptly, the carnage ceased. Marcus and his men, wielding sawn-off shotguns and Uzis, cautiously crouched behind the expansive bar, waiting, watching. No sound; nothing but a gaunt quiet remained. Then, just as suddenly, several armed figures all clad in black burst into the room.

"Fire!" Marcus shouted, not hesitating for a moment.

The intruders were caught completely off guard as the bikers let loose with an incredible onslaught of bullets, firing indiscriminately at anything that moved in front of them. Whether the intruders were wearing body armor or not made no difference as they were brutally cut down at close range. Even after all had fallen, the drunk biker kept firing, laughing and screaming in equal measure.

"Enough!" Marcus called out, though the drunk ignored him. Marcus stepped across and yanked the gun from his intoxicated friend. "I said that's enough."

The acrid smell of gun powder hung in the air. So did the reek of death.

"Bill, Bobby," Marcus said, "go check if that's all of them. And be careful."

The two nodded and did as they were ordered, carefully stepping over the bodies littered around them, and exited the room, their guns raised.

Marcus rounded the bar at last and carefully examined the corpses lying there. All were dead, gruesomely so, including some of his own men. The intruders all looked the same, wearing identical all-black outfits, all brandishing the same weapon—the ever popular AK-47. Clearly professionals. No markings or identification of any kind.

"That's all of them," Bill, a much younger and less muscular version of Marcus, said, reappearing at the door. "They crashed in with some sort of small armored vehicle. At least twenty of our boys down. And...and..."

"And?" Marcus said impatiently.

"Maggie, she's..."

"Oh no," Marcus said, allowing emotion into his voice, something he never did under normal situations. The only emotion he ever exhibited in front of his men was anger. Fear and intimidation is what kept him on top and what held the group together.

Marcus streaked out into the clubhouse lobby, blood and mangled bodies scattered everywhere. He slipped in a puddle of red on the tiled floor, but managed to lurch towards the staircase, leaping up three at a time. What he saw at the top turned his stomach and brought him to his knees. His pregnant wife, Maggie, lay there in a crumpled heap, blood everyplace. The intruders had given no mercy. He cradled her head in his lap, tried to wipe the blood and red-streaked hair from her face, but he couldn't escape the ruddy stuff. On the floor, on his hands, his torso, all over his wife's torn and lifeless body. He couldn't escape from the crimson nightmare.

"Maggie," Marcus whispered.

He caressed her, then let out an unholy wail, tears streaming down his face. Then he was done. He gently laid his wife down and retreated back toward the bar.

"Marcus," Bill said as his leader entered the bar, "who were these punks? Cops?"

"They're not cops," Marcus said harshly. "Cops don't come barging in firing at will without cause. Cops carry ID. This is Latham's people, ordered here by whoever's now in charge over there."

"Latham?" Bobby said, a much more clean-cut biker compared with all the others. "You think?"

"They're not giving up their turf without a fight. Well, I'll give them a fight. One they'll never forget." Marcus turned, his back now facing his comrades. "This city is gonna burn."

* * * * * *

Bob Sloan sat at his desk and reread the text message he had received from The Wraith the previous day. It concerned him...a lot. Crossfire back in Metro City. The thought sent shivers down his spine. The city was in serious trouble if they couldn't nab the assassin and quickly.

"There you go again," Sloan heard Perez say. He looked up and noticed her seated at her desk in front of his. He could have sworn she wasn't there a moment ago.

"What?" he said.

"You and that phone of yours. Zoning out. What gives?"

Sloan briefly paused before speaking. "I know who's responsible for the attacks, the murders of both Latham and Grieco."

"How can you possibly know that?" Perez pressed. "I've seen the same evidence as you, perused the same crime scenes. There's nothing to indicate anyone, or have I missed something. Are you holding out on me?"

"Trust me, Perez, but I know."

"How? C'mon, how?"

Sloan squirmed in his seat.

"Okay, indulge me, enlighten me with this fascinating truth you're not dying to tell me," Perez said, dripping with sarcasm and skepticism.

Sloan leaned forward over his desk and whispered, "It's Crossfire."

"What?" Perez said, a little louder than both he and she would have wanted under the circumstances. She, too, leaned forward. "That's not possible. He was killed, The..." She stopped herself before whimpering, "...told me."

"The Wraith?" Sloan said, smiling. "Who do you think told me Crossfire's not only alive but back in Metro City? He's behind everything."

"No way," Perez said, confusion written all over her face. "No way. How is this possible?"

"I don't know, but at least we now know who we're dealing with."

"But we have no evidence, Bob, nothing to prove Crossfire's our man let alone back from the dead. You know how this works, or is supposed to. Evidence, we need evidence."

"I trust The Wraith."

Perez flopped back into her chair, clearly trying to take it all in. Ultimately, she said, "What is it with you and The Wraith? First you're leading a one-man army against him, and now...now you're practically his sidekick or something."

Sloan smiled again and tapped his nose. "I've learned some things and understood some things. Let's leave it at that. But I trust the man and what he's trying to do for this city."

"All right then, if you say so," Perez said. "I was always pro-Wraith, pretty much right from the start. I want that on the record here."

"I know, I know," Sloan said. "Okay, so we know who we're dealing with. What now?"

"You tell me," Perez said. "You're the one with The Wraith's phone number."

Sloan ignored her barb and opened a stuffed manila folder on his desk. "That scum must have left some evidence somewhere. Go over everything we know about the case so far, over every witness testimony we have. Any other crimes in the city that may lead back to him. Someone must know something."

Perez sighed, but followed her partner's lead. It was going to be a long day.

* * * * * *

Paul sat in his antique brown leather wing chair in his study at home, enjoying a cup of coffee, trying to take Leena's advice and just relax. Furnished and designed in the style of the Victorian and Edwardian eras, with deep brown and mahogany, there were two mighty bookshelves filled with monographs of every description, and various priceless landscape paintings adorned the vacant walls. This was where Paul felt most at home and comfortable.

Draining his cup, he moved over to the large buffet to his left and refilled it from the Keurig capsule machine, which sat to the left alongside a series of crystal decanters filled with a variety of the very best examples of Sherry, Scotch, and Cognac. The latest edition of the *Metro City Times* newspaper lay beside the coffee machine. Paul grabbed it and took it, along with his cup and saucer, back to the chair. He got comfortable before nearly spitting his coffee out when he saw the headline news. It read:

FLYING HERO SWOOPS! SAVES DOZENS FROM TRAIN WRECK!

And there was a small, but clear, photo to prove it. Calls himself "Starflame" and is apparently here to help, or so the man says. It was all there in black and white.

Paul dropped the paper in his lap, scratched his head and tousled his short, brown hair. This was something he'd have to look into as soon as things were cleared up in Metro.

Cleared up...that's a laugh, he thought. *Since when is this city ever not in some sort of peril? Even when Leena and I tried to take a vacation, we barely had five minutes of rest before all hell broke loose. At least I managed to find the time to propose to her. Just when we'll find the time for a wedding is anyone's guess.*

It was no good. He found it impossible to relax as Leena had implored him to do, not while Crossfire was still at large, no doubt planning his next atrocity. He had to do something.

With a steely determination, he stood and strode over to his Blackwood desk, removed a small remote control device from the right-hand top drawer and pressed a button on it. Instantly, with a slight whooshing of gears, a section of the wide bookcase to the side of the desk shifted forward and then slid effortlessly to one side, revealing the secret entrance to his Lair. He stepped into the darkness whereupon the bookcase eased back into place automatically behind him.

Moving forward onto the upper level, powerful overhead lights strobed on, bathing the entire Lair with a crisp, white brightness. The Lair stood in stark contrast to the Sanderson home. Whereas the mansion was old-style money, featuring antique architecture and furnishings, the Lair was futuristic, all chrome and tile. Equipped with the very latest in technology and fitness paraphernalia, this was where Paul worked, where his war on crime began and ended.

He sat at his computer terminal and brought up the file he had on Crossfire. It wasn't much as the villain had been adept at covering his tracks over the years, making much of his past life nothing but an infernal mystery. Whatever information Paul had been able to unearth, however, was here, including everything about their previous encounter. It was a slim chance, but perusing all he knew about Crossfire might yield something of value to aid him now.

The door's mechanism shook Paul from his thoughts. He turned and noticed Simpson appearing on the Lair's upper deck.

"Yes, Simpson?"

"An invitation, sir," the butler replied, descending via the small elevator. "I thought you'd want to see this immediately."

A compact silver tray was balanced in Simpson's right hand, which he extended toward Paul, who took the envelope that lay upon it. He tore it open and read its contents carefully.

"What are they thinking?" Paul found himself uttering some moments later.

"Excuse me, sir?"

"I've been invited to a charity black tie gala...by Mr. Robert Latham."

* * * * * *

Perez scanned each document with a meticulous precision. She never undertook any duty with anything less than one hundred and ten percent of effort, or so she liked to describe it. It was just her way. Always had been.

"Hmm..." Perez said. "This could be something."

"What have you found?" Sloan said, not bothering to lift his head from his own reading.

"A cabbie was murdered a little while back, his body dumped in the trunk of his own cab. The vehicle was left in the city's outskirts and set alight."

"Dammit," Sloan muttered. "The one remotely possible lead we've managed to come up with and it goes nowhere."

"I take it you've found nothing?"

"Zip, nada, zilch."

"So, you think Crossfire killed that cab driver, then?"

"I think it's at least possible," Sloan said, taking a deep breath. "I sure would have liked to have looked further into that."

Perez noticed her partner's deep frustration.

"Damn!" Sloan said harshly, slamming his manila folder onto his desk. "Crossfire knows how to cover his tracks."

"We'll get him, Bob. He'll slip up somewhere along the line."

"Sloan, Perez. We need to talk about security arrangements," Commissioner Harrison said, exiting his office.

"Security, sir?" Perez asked.

"Oh no, don't tell me," Sloan moaned.

"Latham Industries has decided to move ahead with the charity gala. And we're all invited, by no less than Robert Latham himself."

~ Chapter 11 ~

"You're holding a what?"

"A charity gala," Azufi stammered. "Invitations had already been sent out before I knew anything about it. It was all being organized by Mr. Latham himself. I had very little knowledge of—"

Crossfire lashed out with a powerful backhand, connecting with the side of Azufi's face, sending the hapless businessman hurtling to the floor.

"I'm in charge of this business. Everything now goes through me, do you understand?" Crossfire shrieked in uncharacteristic fury.

Azufi weakly sat up, gently rubbed at his sore cheek. He wondered if any bones had been broken. "I...I'm sorry, I..."

"Shut up. Your babbling is giving me a headache," Crossfire grunted, before his demeanor completely changed.

"But this will be the perfect opportunity to play with my enemy's mind. He'll never expect me to be at this gala."

Azufi shakily got to his feet, his head swimming. "You attend the gala? Are you insane?"

Crossfire whirled at that, a fierce anger writ large upon his face, but which quickly faded into a creepy, disturbing smile. His threatened violence dissolved instantly.

"You can't be seen in public, you can't be associated with me in any way," Azufi said.

Crossfire lifted a hand as though about to strike, causing Azufi to flinch and whimper, but he held back once again.

"Do as you're told," Crossfire finally said as he sat at Azufi's desk, continuing to smile. "This gala will be the perfect moment to further torment The Wraith. Mental anguish as well as physical torture. He won't escape my vengeance."

Azufi couldn't make any sense of Crossfire's ravings, but one thing he *was* sure of—Crossfire's behavior was beginning to change. He had no idea how or why, but it was perceptible, and becoming moreso with each passing day.

And becoming more terrifying.

* * * * * *

"Okay, Bob, you were right."

Sloan cupped his right ear, grinning as he did so. "I didn't hear you. Could you please repeat that?"

"Yeah, okay," Perez said, a little chagrined. "I was hoping the cab wasn't completely destroyed, but..."

The two detectives looked at the recovered remains of the torched cab, which had been collected and deposited at the council depot some blocks from their precinct. All around them and the cab were city equipment used for trash collection, landscaping, and street cleaning. Workmen milled about, completely ignoring the two cops as they stared at the blackened wreck.

"So, now what?" Perez asked.

"What do we know about the driver?" Sloan asked, fiddling with his baseball cap. "When was he last seen alive? What was his usual route?"

"As I recall," Perez started, "his name was Toby Martin. Middle-aged, married, grandkids. Drove all over the city, but was primarily based out of the city airport. Was last seen alive the morning of August tenth by his wife."

"Two months back," Sloan mused. "Grieco was killed about a month ago. All seems to fit."

"What's that?"

"Oh, I'm just theorizing, Perez. The timeline fits. If this driver was killed by Crossfire, it would make sense. He flies back into town, the driver picks him up, maybe found out too much. Exit Toby Martin. And then Grieco cops it a few weeks later. Both victims killed and their bodies dumped elsewhere."

"That really gets us nowhere, Bob," Perez said, her hands on her hips. "That sounds like just about every murderer with half a brain. Sure, it makes sense, but it proves nothing without the data to back it up."

"I know," Sloan said in exasperation, "but my gut is talking to me again and I've never failed to listen to it. We're onto something here, I can feel it."

Perez raised an eyebrow. "We better get back to the station. We have to prepare for that charity thing tomorrow."

"Don't remind me," Sloan fired back, rolling his eyes.

They promptly headed for the depot exit to begin their journey back to the precinct.

* * * * * *

The following day, Paul sat fitfully in the Lair, continuing to brood over the situation, the lack of progress in the fight against Crossfire. It galled him to admit the next move was Crossfire's as he'd stated earlier, but it was nevertheless true. Without any clue as to where his enemy was hiding himself and what he was up to, all Paul could do was to wait. And be ready.

"Hmm..." he said to himself. "This is interesting."

He was again reading through the file detailing all that was known about Crossfire and their previous skirmish when something of interest finally caught his eye, a small footnote detailing a certain object of antiquity.

"Found something?"

"What? Leena!"

His fiancé had managed to enter the Lair and approach him without his knowledge so engrossed was he with his researches. He had taught her well.

"Sorry, did I startle you?" Leena said with some amusement.

"Just concentrating. I didn't hear you come in."

Leena smiled. "Which brings me back to my question. What have you found?"

Paul smiled back at her. "Look at this. Remember the Monete Della Trinita, the Coins of the Trinity?"

"How could I forget," Leena said, clearly concentrating her memory. "Three gold coins supposedly gifted to the baby Jesus by the Three Wise Men. Two were destroyed nearly one hundred years ago. One remained, which Robert Latham tried to possess, apparently with the idea that it would grant him immortality."

"Right," Paul said, impressed by Leena's quick recall. "We determined all that the last time we faced Crossfire. But look here" —he pointed at a paragraph on the computer screen in front of him— "I've delved deeper into the history of the coins and managed to come up with this tidbit. Another aspect of the legend hitherto unbeknownst to us. While possession of the remaining coin does apparently grant one immortality, it's predicated on the coin remaining constantly in their custody."

"But why didn't we discover this information before?" Leena asked. "Why are we only finding this out now?"

"It's in an ancient form of Aramaic that our previous computer system failed to decipher. And thus we overlooked it entirely."

"Okay," Leena said, "so one is immortal only while holding the coin. Where does that lead us?"

"It goes on to say that prolonged possession of the coin leads to behavioral changes and, ultimately, madness. Only the strongest of wills can withstand the power of the coin for any length of time." He sat back and took a deep breath. "Looks like the price of immortality is complete insanity."

Leena gasped at the revelation.

Paul swiveled in his chair. "This explains two things to me. This is how Crossfire survived being shot by Grieco years ago—he was holding the coin at the time; and it explains his errors of judgment now. Clearly, he still has the coin, which makes him an even deadlier threat to this city. There's no telling what he might do in his mad quest for revenge against me. And with the coin still in his control, it might be impossible to stop him."

Leena's gaze met Paul's as they contemplated this terrible realization. Moments passed in awkward silence before Leena ultimately snapped out of it.

"Oh, I nearly forgot why I came down here in the first place," she said. "It's time to get ready."

"Ready?"

"It's the night of the gala, remember?"

Hours later, the classic Daimler pulled to a stop outside the impressive, Brutalist designed Metro City Convention Center. Paul and Leena exited the car to be met by a barrage of flash bulbs and paparazzi. The center itself had been surrounded by a high, barbed wire fence, with guards and police officers peppering the perimeter. Paul saw Sloan milling about outside, so Perez was no doubt also somewhere. Security, clearly, was at the forefront of everyone's thinking this time around.

Paul smoothed his hand down the trousers of his immaculately fitting bespoke tuxedo. He extended an arm toward his fiancé, who eagerly took it.

"You look stunning, Mrs. Sanderson," Paul said with a wink.

Leena did indeed look ravishing in a svelte, blue Alex Perry designed gown. "Why thank you, Mr. Sanderson," she replied with a smile. "But I'm not Mrs. Sanderson yet."

"We should work on that."

"Name a date," Leena said with vigor.

Paul was about to reply when the line on the red carpet they had entered proceeded in front of them. They then reached the first security checkpoint. Armed, plain-clothed security guards stood impassively on either side of the gate. Paul handed one of them their invitation, which the guard passed through a compact handheld scanner. A melodic beep, a green light, and they were on their way. Neither guard smiled or said one word.

"Friendly bunch," Leena quipped.

Now within the grounds of the center, the two continued their march, two-by-two, along with dozens of other well-dressed couples, and some not so well-dressed.

It was slow going, for the path laid out for them was a narrow one, with the same high wire fence towering on either side, but eventually Paul and Leena reached the building's broad front entrance. Emblazoned banners above it indicated the charity in question and yet more guards ushered them into the lobby. Once inside, they were faced with a series of still more guards, all dressed in the same black suits as the others, and a giant overhead metal detector and body scanner that everyone had to pass through. It left Metro City's airport, Melton Memorial, for dead security wise.

As soon as they had been prodded, scanned, and their possessions X-rayed, they were finally allowed to proceed and enter the main auditorium. The center presented a different picture on the inside. Whereas outside the scene resembled something one might have found in Communist Russia or East Berlin—harsh and cold—the interior proved the exact opposite. Here it was warm, colorful, brightly decorated and lit, and filled with a raucous crowd of, apparently, happy people. Soft music floated on the air. Clearly, the murder of Robert Latham and the attacks on the city hadn't dampened the wealthy's enthusiasm for a free party.

They began to mingle. Paul noticed Commissioner Harrison by the refreshment table, where drinks from the bar were being served, and waved to him. Mayor Hutchison could be seen bobbing and weaving amongst the throng, no doubt lapping up the attention and likely receiving congratulations and thanking any donors to his campaign for his electoral success. There, too, was Patrich Azufi, well-dressed as always but looking somewhat diminished, Paul thought. The businessman's pallor wasn't good and he wore too much mousse in his hair.

"Paul Sanderson," a horribly familiar voice emanated from behind him. "How wonderful to *meet* you at last."

Paul whirled. Leena couldn't suppress a gasp. There stood Crossfire, dressed to the nine's as the rest of them, a broad smile on his face and holding out his hand, thrusting it into Paul's and shaking it vigorously. They both squeezed with all their might, neither wishing to yield, neither wishing to give any sign of weakness.

Paul weakly smiled, tried to compose himself. "Pleasure to meet you, Mr...?"

"Smith," Crossfire said. "Call me Smith."

"Mr. Smith, then," Paul started before whispering, "what are you doing here, Crossfire? Haven't you had enough of your game playing?"

"Mr. Sanderson," Crossfire said with a chuckle, "I've only just started. I have lots more in train for you and this city."

"What's stopping me from taking you in right now?" Paul said softly albeit through gritted teeth. Leena could but only watch the verbal cat and mouse battle with horror, the tension palpable.

"You could try, but I doubt you'd succeed. Besides, I don't think you'd want to jeopardize your little...secret identity."

"I'd risk anything to put you away," Paul said fervently. "Even that."

"Risk anything?" Crossfire said with some mirth. "Even the lives of everyone here?"

"What are you talking about?" Paul spat.

"Nothing of consequence," Crossfire said, his grotesque, arrogant smile never leaving him. "Just a little TNT placed throughout this building, enough to take us all sky high and then some. I have the controls right here." He produced a small remote control device from his pocket.

Paul eyed it through narrow slits.

"Careful now," Crossfire said, placing the device back into his pocket, "it might accidentally go off."

Paul was furious and felt the steam rising within him but he was powerless to do anything. Crossfire couldn't help himself, gloating and chuckling all at once.

"The vaunted Dread Avenger. Pah! You're nothing. And once I'm through with you, this city will know it. The whole world will know it." The villain threw up a hand in a feigned, foppish way. "Enjoy the party. Drinks are over there."

He left the two of them, slowly walking away and disappeared into the crowd.

"I can't believe he showed up here," Leena said finally. "I can't believe he'd take such a risk."

"The braggart," Paul said in a foul tone. "He knew just about everyone here wouldn't know him, wouldn't be able to identify him, and he took precautions against any actions I might have taken against him as well."

Leena looked at him with deep concern in her features.

"But you're right," Paul continued. "It was still a heck of a risk. Sloan and Perez are outside. They could identify him, perhaps other cops as well. And to have access to place his explosives, which makes me think..."

"He's got a link to the inside," Leena said, reading his mind. "Azufi?"

"Could be," Paul said. "It bears further investigation, certainly. I'm confident of one thing, though—the coin has done its handiwork. Crossfire is clearly not thinking straight. He's become overconfident, starting to make multiple mistakes. Speaking of the coin..."

Paul pulled from his pocket a gold coin, the very coin in question. It was a little larger than expected, and ornately decorated on either side in a Romanesque fashion. It was oddly hypnotic, capturing one's gaze, and was in surprisingly good condition considering its age.

"That's not....How on Earth?" Leena gasped, looking at the coin with a visible mix of awe and horror.

"I took something of a risk of my own," Paul said. "While Crossfire was rapt in his own glory, I was able to pick his pockets and found this." Paul twirled the coin in his fingers, the gold catching the light and shining at odd angles. It was a marvel to behold.

"This is a dangerous artifact to own," Leena said at last, "if the legend is true."

"With prolonged exposure, for want of a better description, comes madness. You're right, but we're safe for the time being. I think it likely Crossfire has already passed the point of no return, though. Quickly now, let's merge with the crowd and discreetly exit. We have a lot of work to do tonight."

Leena appeared confused at this, but joined Paul as they quietly made their way away from the festivities.

~ Chapter 12 ~

Back in the Lair, Paul and Leena were joined by Max, who was examining the coin under his scope.

"Remarkable," the Irishman said with enthusiasm. "Truly remarkable. To think, this was a gift to the Christ child. That Jesus Himself may have actually touched this."

"It's amazing to think about," Paul said a little impatiently, his bow tie untied and hanging loose around his neck, "but what can you tell us about it?"

"What can I say?" Max said, lifting his head at last. "It's an old, gold coin. Nothing different in its construction than any other coin of the period, though it's in superb condition for something that is over two thousand years old. Look at how it shines."

"We thought the same thing," Leena said.

"But there's nothing else?" Paul asked.

"Nothing," Max said. "Its significance is in its provenance not with what it's made of."

Paul turned, rubbed his chin in deep thought. "Max," he spoke some moments later, "is this something you can forge? I need a precise replica. Tonight!"

* * * * * *

It was close to midnight as Azufi slithered into his office at work. The party was still going strong back at the convention center, but he could no longer stomach it. He certainly didn't feel like having fun. Not anymore.

He hated being back in his poky old office. It was cramped and uncomfortable. As the current head of the organization, he felt he deserved better. But, really, he was no longer the head. Not with Crossfire looming over him at every turn. Work had become a chore, and home was no longer a comfort for him. Whenever he was stressed on the job, he would go home to get some action, but that, too, had been taken from him by Crossfire. So what then was left? Nothing. He felt like weeping.

"Wha...what's that?" he found himself saying aloud.

There, on the carpet by the door, something sparkling in the low light. Curious, he went there and picked it up. It was a coin, a gold coin. Azufi turned it over in his hand. He hadn't seen anything like this anywhere other than in a museum. It was heavy and appeared very old yet strangely almost completely untarnished. Where had it come from? Nobody but himself and the cleaning staff had access to this room. Nobody but...

"What are you doing with that!" Crossfire screamed as he barged into the office, causing Azufi to stumble back in surprise. "Where did you get that? How dare you!"

"What? This?" Azufi said in shock, holding the coin aloft.

Crossfire saw the coin up close and exploded with anger, tearing the coin from Azufi's grasp with one hand and launching a powerful blow with the other. Azufi had no chance to avoid it, taking the punch to the side of his jaw. It nearly took his head off. He violently fell back, landing hard against his desk, the edge of which caught him in the kidneys, sending him to his knees. He coughed in pain, blood flowing from his mouth, the small of his back and his knees aching.

"How dare you touch this!" Crossfire madly screeched. "How did you get this? How? I thought I'd lost this!"

Azufi coughed up more blood, struggled to answer. "I...I found it here...on the carpet."

"Found it? *Found it?*"

There was no respite to Crossfire's fury, his insanity. He had the coin in his right hand, turned it over multiple times, as Azufi watched on helplessly, in mortal fear for his life.

"FOUND IT!" Crossfire screamed at the top of his lungs, seemingly losing control over himself, grappling with his emotions almost as though he was waging an intense war within his very soul. Crossfire gripped his head, grunted as though he was in as much pain as Azufi.

Azufi struggled to his feet, needed to prop himself against his desk as his knees gave way beneath him. The small of his back felt like it was on fire and his face, too, felt red hot. He could barely stand.

"Crossfire, listen," Azufi wheezed as he shuffled forward. He had to get away, had to escape this monster. "I don't know what's wrong, or what that coin means to you, but..."

Crossfire released his head and stared at Azufi, who stopped cold as a result. Sweat poured from Crossfire's brow, his features wildly contorted. He lashed out again, catching

Azufi in the midriff with his boot, again sending the hapless businessman to his knees.

Crossfire stood over Azufi, his body shaking, unable to stay still. Azufi managed to catch sight of his attacker gazing at the coin as though in a trance. Moments passed, then Crossfire grunted and stormed from the office as darkness hovered over Azufi.

* * * * * *

The Wraith crouched atop the Latham Industries building. Via the bug he had earlier planted in Azufi's office, when he had also placed the replica coin there, he had heard everything—Azufi's discovery of the coin, Crossfire's madness rearing its presence, and their violent confrontation. His theory of a connection between the two had been spot-on.

He mused on what Leena had told him. The coin certainly was a dangerous artifact to own. Even without the genuine article in his possession, Crossfire's mental state was badly degrading. The Wraith felt there was little hope for Crossfire now. But, in that moment, he had more important things to think about. Crossfire had left Azufi's office and was likely to head to his bolthole now that he thought he recovered his asset—the coin. The Wraith had to be ready to follow.

He pulled his night-vision binoculars from his belt and scanned the roadside beneath him. He couldn't dare lose his enemy now. For some minutes, there was little sign of life in the streets below. But then, after some further tense moments waiting, there was movement. The Wraith zoomed in with his scope. It was Crossfire, heading for a compact car. This was it. He had to act fast.

The Wraith produced his grapnel gun and attached a small homing device within its barrel. Without a moment to lose, he aimed and fired. The tiny device, in the shape of the Eyes of Judgment, found its mark, attaching soundly on the car's rear bumper.

Crossfire sped away, the compact spewing a thick, black smoke from its exhaust. The Wraith returned his binoculars to its pouch and allowed himself a brief smile. Soon there would be a reckoning and Crossfire would be held accountable for his actions.

* * * * * *

The impressive, fully appointed black limousine came to a slow halt in the drive of the Azufi home.

"Do you need some help inside, Mr. Azufi?" the driver, a young man eager to please, asked.

"No...no, I'll be fine, Smithers," Azufi feebly said, trying in vain to stifle a cough of pain. His right eye was almost completely swollen shut, his face was lightly smeared with blood where he had missed it while cleaning himself earlier, and his forehead was smudged with hair mousse that had run down his head. His white dinner shirt was spotted with blood. He could have gone to the doctor. Perhaps he should have, but all he wanted to do was go home and go to sleep. Possibly in the morning...

With a deep breath, he slowly opened the car's rear door and took a tentative step out. He grunted in pain as he tried to stand fully erect, the small of his back erupting in spasms of pain. Azufi hunched forward in an effort to alleviate the pressure. It didn't help much.

"Are you sure you don't need some assistance, sir?" Smithers asked again.

"Leave me alone," Azufi snapped. He wasn't in the mood to be mollycoddled.

He began to awkwardly shuffle up the drive toward his house, but it was slow going. The house felt like it was ten miles away.

Why didn't that fool drop me off closer? Azufi mulled with some annoyance.

He heard the limo reversing behind him and wondered, briefly, if he should have taken Smithers up on his offer. He'd be inside his home by now, ready to collapse into bed and hope for a better tomorrow. He didn't have the energy to try and signal his driver and so pressed on. He managed another three tortured steps before he needed to catch his breath. He damned his current situation, damned Crossfire for doing this to him. He looked up at his house. It still seemed so far away. He bowed his head, determined to continue.

A cracking sound from the bushes at the far end of his front yard caught his attention, but then a mighty explosion tore through his house, causing Azufi to fall backward, harshly landing on his tailbone.

He craned his neck up with some difficulty. Flames were spewing up and outward in every direction. Debris lay all around him; a burning block of timber had careened from the house and had missed him by mere inches.

Azufi tried to sit up, tried to make sense of what had just taken place, but he was in too much pain, and his mind was in too much of a jumble.

"You were supposed to die," a deep, menacing voice sliced through the inky darkness to his right.

Without seeing anything, Azufi could still recognize the extreme danger he was currently in. He desperately clawed at the ground. He needed to get to his feet, needed to flee. It couldn't end here, not like this.

A tall man, dressed in black leather and blue denim emerged from the night, coming into the weak light and walking toward Azufi. He was followed by another similarly clothed burly individual. Upon reaching Azufi, the lead man crouched down, a long red ponytail coming into view, and he closely eyed Azufi with piercing blue eyes.

"You? You're running Latham's organization now? You've got to be kidding me," the man said.

"Wha...wha..." was all Azufi managed to utter in response.

The tall stranger kicked Azufi in the stomach. Azufi coughed furiously, unable to breath and in serious pain.

"You killed my wife!" the tall stranger yelled as he kicked Azufi in the stomach once again. This time Azufi felt something pop inside him, and he felt a pain unlike any he had experienced before. He struggled to remain conscious. He knew he was in trouble. Deep trouble.

"I want you to know the name of the man you've wronged and who has dealt with you in return," the tall stranger said, again crouching beside Azufi. "I'm Marcus Redding. Leader of the Bandidos, and you're about to—"

Police sirens wailed close by.

"C'mon, Marcus, we gotta get outta here," Marcus's fellow gang member said, grabbing Marcus by the arm.

Azufi managed to catch a glimpse of the two men receding back into the shadows as the sirens grew louder and blurred flashes of red appeared.

"Help me," Azufi struggled to whisper. "Help me."

Then, nothing. Darkness reigned.

* * * * * *

SOMEWHERE SECRET – FOUR YEARS EARLIER

The darkness was all enveloping. As she slowly opened her eyes a fraction, she could scarcely tell any difference between the two environments. She had difficulty fully opening her eyes as though they were glued shut. With some considerable effort, she awoke more fully and attempted to sit up. She realized where she had lain was rock hard, and her body ached all over. She could see nothing in the pitch dark. She had no idea where she was.

Images suddenly flashed through her mind, wild and violent memories she couldn't make sense of, and forgot the instant they disappeared. She gripped her head in shock more than in pain. What was going on. No wait. There was a struggle...high above the ground...with...with...

Nothing. She could remember nothing. Fleeting moments appeared and then disappeared without recognition, without clarification. She couldn't even remember her own name. Panic began to rise up inside her. She needed to run, to get away, to think.

Powerful overhead lights abruptly blazed on, blinding her. She shielded her eyes to give them time to adjust to the brightness, to seeing anything at all. Slowly, she could now discern her surroundings. To her left, she was horrified to discover a large pentagram on the wall, with what appeared to be the image of some sort of goat-like man within it. Test tubes and beakers filled with all sorts of—creatures?—littered the tables and chairs around her. She tried to move forward, but found it difficult to walk. Her muscles felt weak as though she hadn't used them for a long time. But how was that possible? It was then she noticed she wore little more than a hospital gown. She was cold, shivered a little.

"Ah, my goodness, you are awake, my child," a serpent-like voice said. The man who spoke stood in the now-open doorway before her. He was short, a little pudgy, with white hair and eyebrows, the latter of which arched upwards at the ends, giving the man a devilish sort of appearance. He seemed to almost slither into the room.

"This is unexpected," he said. "I hadn't expected you to awaken for quite some time."

"Who...who are you?" she struggled to say, her vocal chords feeling stiff and uneasy. "Who am I?"

"Oh, my child," he said, attempting to sound warm and sympathetic but not succeeding at either. "My name is Dr. Standish. I'm here to help you. You were badly injured over a year ago. I have been...helping you, working on you."

Working on me? That didn't sound right at all. *A year? A year!*

She looked around herself, seeing more horrifying images of devilry and witchcraft. That settled it. She needed to escape, felt the urge to flee more strongly than ever.

"Don't touch me," she shrieked as he tried to grab her by the arm. She was stronger now, her limbs filled with an energy that felt both natural and...different somehow. She latched on to Standish's arm and yanked him to one side in an effort to push past him and get to the door. She was astonished to see Standish fly into the shelves to her left, crashing and sending broken glass and...things...down onto the floor.

She momentarily stood there, stunned by what she had just done, by the strength she had just shown and somehow knew she never had before. She had just flung aside a full grown man as though he was a rag doll.

Standish groaned a little, gripping his head. She breathed a sigh of relief knowing he was okay, but then the urge to escape came back to her. She had to get away.

"Natalya," Standish wheezed as she reached the door. "Natalya. You need to stay with me. My work is not yet complete."

That name—She stopped cold, stood rigid. That name meant something to her. Didn't it? She struggled with her mind and emotions. All ran wild, but in the end, nothing came. The name ultimately felt like it applied to someone else. Someone long dead.

She glanced at Standish one last time before bolting through the open doorway and making good on her escape.

*　*　*　*　*　*

The Wraith checked his watch. It was 2AM. He was positioned on the roof of a warehouse opposite another such building where Crossfire's car was parked. An eerie, salty fog rolled over from the Atlantic.

Clever devil, he thought. *This was one of his hideouts the last time he menaced Metro City. He knew this would be one of the last places anyone would ever think to look for him.*

He examined the opposite rooftop carefully, noticed it closely aligned with his current vantage point at the far end to his right. He made his way there and leapt forward, landing deftly on the corrugated iron and tile roof on the other side.

He scanned the proximity with care. When dealing with an enemy like Crossfire, one couldn't be too careful. If he was to succeed, the element of surprise had to be maintained. As far as he could see, there were no security cameras or devices extant. Clearly, Crossfire was not expecting any company. The Wraith would use that over-confidence to his advantage.

He inched forward toward a massive and grimy skylight and peered through it. Years of dust and cobwebs blighted his view, but he could still make out someone moving on the floor below. Yes, it was Crossfire. The villain paced back and forth at speed. The Wraith could see a shelf off to the side with some sort of equipment packed on it and a small table in the center of the room with a laptop on it.

The Wraith clenched his jaw. He vowed there and then this would be their final battle. Crossfire wouldn't escape him this time.

~ Chapter 13 ~

Leena paced up and down alongside Max as he worked on maintaining various pieces of The Wraith's equipment. He smiled, noticing her relentless backward and forward motion. She was more like the Chief than he had previously realized.

"Leena, what's the matter?" Max finally asked, halting his progress on a Wraith uniform.

"I'm worried about Paul. He intends tonight to be his and Crossfire's last encounter. With Crossfire as mad as he is..."

"The Chief can take care of himself," Max said in a relaxed fashion. "You know that better than anyone. And besides, he has the coin with him. He's practically unstoppable now."

Leena stopped her pacing and looked at Max with some concern. "The coin is the most worrying aspect to all of this. I don't want Paul ending up an insane lunatic."

"It would take months, maybe even years, before that would occur, at least if Crossfire is anything to go by. But enough of that." He lifted the suit he had been working on up to show Leena. "Look at what I've created for you."

"Another Wraith costume?" Leena asked with some curiosity. "But I already have one. You made it so I could mimic Paul's body shape and voice to take his place when needed. Has something happened to that suit?"

"I know, and that suit's fine and dandy, but I've often thought you might like one of your very own, to strike out on your own."

Leena's eyes bulged as she examined the suit more closely. It was similar in design to Paul's, but far more form-fitting, and more stylized, with a lady's shape in mind. The Eyes of Judgment were there as well, but they were not just a design element.

"My own Eyes of Judgment?" Leena queried. "How is that possible?"

"Ahh..." Max said with some pleasure. He always enjoyed talking about his work. "This is the piece de resistance of my little invention, the crème de la crème. Naturally, you lack the powers of the Chief's Judgment Stare so I thought up this useful replacement. Now, listen carefully."

Leena was rapt with attention, sitting down in a chair in front of Max.

"I've managed to combine two very powerful LED lights with my patented flash powder in a way that...well, it's too complicated to explain how I did it, but the bottom line is, by pressing two buttons on your belt, one on each side of the buckle, you can either blind your enemies or fry them."

"Blind them? Fry them?"

"Only temporarily blind them, but very useful in apprehending or defeating difficult opponents. When you press the button on the left of your belt buckle, you activate the flash powder additive and, poof, no more baddie."

Leena appeared amazed at this. He'd rendered her speechless.

"Remember," Max continued, "right button blind, left button fry."

Leena stood and took the suit from Max, holding it aloft. A big smile grew on her face.

"This is brilliant, Max. You've truly outdone yourself."

Max swelled with pride at hearing that. He had to admit, he was pretty chuffed at his achievement as well.

"Any limits on the flash powder?" Leena asked.

"The Eyes link to the capsules in your belt, so when they run dry, no more fry." Max chuckled. "But I wouldn't imagine that happening very often. The LEDs are guaranteed to function long term, and I've encased them in a protective layer of Evanium, so they'll never shatter. They flip open to eject the flash powder when the relevant button is pressed."

"Evanium? Good grief, what's that?"

"Oh," Max chuckled again, "that's an extra strong Perspex I've been developing. Clear as glass, just as thin, but virtually unbreakable."

"Amazing," Leena breathed. "You're a marvel, Max."

He smiled broadly, took the suit back from her and laid it out flat on his workbench.

"Now," he said. "All we have to do is come up with a name for you. How does Lady Wraith grab you?"

* * * * * *

Crossfire's mind raced. He couldn't stay still and felt an overpowering urge to keep moving, to do something, anything. He had recovered the coin; he had achieved his aim in further tormenting his enemy. He was in charge of the largest crime organization on the east coast and he remained, as yet, undiscovered and at liberty. Everything was going his way. So why was he feeling so ill at ease, so tortured? Even he knew he had been behaving oddly in recent days, temper tantrums flaring, outbursts of intense anger, but now...now...

An explosion tore through the ceiling above him, glass raining down like a torrential storm. A cloaked figure of nightmares dropped and appeared before him as though torn from a Faustian vision. The cloak separated, revealing The Wraith, his greatest enemy, now in his sanctuary.

"You?" Crossfire shrieked. "How did you find me? How!"

"I know everything, Crossfire," The Wraith said. "Your involvement with Patrich Azufi, your attempts at wresting control of Latham Industries. It all ends now!"

Crossfire felt a mixture of panic and sheer unadulterated fury flood his body. His rage was uncontrollable.

"How dare you challenge me? You're nothing. *Nothing!*"

They faced each other then in a sort of Mexican standoff, both carefully eyeing each other, ready to act in an instant.

* * * * * *

The face-off stretched on, seconds seeming to last much longer. Then, Crossfire lunged for the shelf unit to his right, the one which was filled with all sorts of weaponry. The Wraith reacted swiftly, producing flash pellets from his belt and lofted them toward the shelf. With a blinding flash, which caught Crossfire completely off guard, all the villain's weapons and equipment—even his protective suit—were disintegrated in seconds.

Crossfire was clearly caught in a mental quagmire. His equipment and weaponry gone, any advantage they might have afforded him negated, he briefly looked lost. He quickly regained his composure, however, and turned to face the Dread Avenger, assuming a fighting stance.

"I don't need all that stuff anyway," Crossfire declared. "I can take you with my bare hands." The villain stood there in his tank top and cargo pants.

The Wraith smiled. "Come try."

Crossfire let out a fierce grunt and then charged, attacking as though he was a Bull Elephant. The Wraith side-swiped Crossfire, stepping to one side and lashing out with a karate chop to the back of the neck. Crossfire crashed to the floor, but was up in an instant, ready to continue the battle.

He charged mindlessly again, letting fly with a series of punches, elbows, and kicks. The Wraith was able to dodge most of them, while his protective suit bore the brunt of the rest. Then it was The Wraith's turn, returning the barrage with a collection of his own. He was determined that this would indeed be their final battle. He was going to fight with everything he had and then some.

He threw a powerful right, connecting with Crossfire's jaw. Then a left, with the same result. And again with a right. And another left. It was like punching a brick wall. The Wraith followed this up with a kick to the stomach and a knee to the face. He didn't dare let up; he knew he had to be swift and powerful and ruthless.

Again and again he pummeled Crossfire with incredible blows to the face and body. Crossfire seemed unable to respond, almost as though his madness had affected his reflexes, slowed him down somehow. Minutes passed and Crossfire now appeared punch-drunk, unable to fight back at all, but unwilling to fall down.

It was then that The Wraith's Eyes of Judgment burst to fiery life, crackling with mystical energy.

"Your time has come," The Wraith moaned. "Time to face proper judgment and be cleansed."

Crossfire was in no position to resist as The Wraith grabbed him by the head and forced him to look into the Eyes. Crossfire's whole body tensed, his eyes bulging open as the powers of the Judgment Stare washed over him, enveloping his very soul. He opened his mouth, but nothing came. The Wraith pressed on, intending to deliver the fullest dose possible to an enemy so evil and so deadly.

A few more moments and it was done. Crossfire lay in a heap on the floor, his hair singed, gibbering like a mindless imbecile. Judgment had been severe.

The Wraith took a moment to catch his breath. The battle had been won but at what cost to Crossfire he knew not. Nevertheless it was now over, and that's all that mattered. He cast his eye about. Leaving his opponent a jittery mess on the floor, The Wraith reconnoitered his surroundings, eager to ensure the entire area was completely secure.

The warehouse's main floor was quickly given the all clear. Next he turned his attention to the office off to the side. Entering this room carefully, what he found there sickened his stomach. A woman lay before him on a filthy cot, her negligee torn and tattered, her near-naked body covered in dried blood and welts. The Wraith had seen the like all too often. It was clear to him that she had been sexually assaulted, and likely more than once.

With tears welling in his eyes, he knelt beside her and felt for a pulse. It was weak but detectable. She was in desperate need of medical attention and The Wraith knew the fastest way was to take her to the nearest hospital himself. He gently scooped her up in his arms and marched from the room where he was greeted with another shock—Crossfire had vanished, his Judgment Stare having proven only partially successful.

Despite this setback, he continued with his mission, exiting the warehouse and strode over to his Rolls, where he lay the woman on the backseat. He noted the hatchback was also missing.

Good, he thought. *I'll be able to track him again. He won't escape me for long.*

Without another thought, he gunned the car to life and roared away.

* * * * * *

"Gottagetawaygottagetmoreweapons," Crossfire babbled incoherently as he madly sped through the city streets. He looked up into the mirror. His face was a bloody pulp and he was practically bald as his scalp was badly burned. His mind raced. He couldn't string two thoughts together, and his very soul was in deep torment. All he knew was he had to get away.

He yanked at the wheel, making a sharp left, clipping another car in the process, causing his own compact to spin out of control. The car crashed into a group of trash cans lining the entrance to a narrow side street and into the building behind. Crossfire desperately tried to restart the car, but it refused to turn over.

"Gottagetawaygottagetaway."

He burst from the car, losing his footing while doing so. He started to sprint. He had to get to Lazar. He had to re-equip himself. To regroup. As addled as his brain was, as rambling as his thoughts were, he nevertheless knew he was only a block or two from his destination. He had to get there as fast as possible. His salvation lay there.

In minutes, he had reached the same dingy restaurant that was Anton Lazar's place of business. He barged through the open door, pushed past the elderly Chinese lady that was still there, and stormed through to the back.

"Mr. Crossfire, sir?" the gunsmith Lazar said with some surprise. "You startled me. What has happened to you?"

"Ineedeverything," Crossfire said wildly. "Everythingyouhave."

"Calm down, please," Lazar pleaded. "What exactly do you require from me?"

Crossfire sharply turned his head this way and that, surveying his surroundings.

"I have a spare uniform for you over here." Lazar pointed over to the packed shelf unit behind him. "As to your other equipment, I would need time to—"

Crossfire didn't let him finish. He pushed past the small man, grabbed the spare uniform, and started pilfering everything he thought of value. Guns, ammo, explosives, nothing was spared.

"Mr. Crossfire, please," Lazar implored, "you cannot take those. They are for my other clients."

Lazar tried to maneuver himself between Crossfire and the shelves of equipment but all that did was further enrage Crossfire, who reacted with a grunt and a backhand punch to Lazar's face, sending the gunsmith spiraling to the floor.

Crossfire continued removing weaponry of every size and description and piled them all up on the main workbench in the center of the room. He then realized he would need help carrying everything and looked about for any sort of bag or sack to do so. On the bottom shelf of the unit opposite were several empty duffel bags. He grabbed those and stuffed each of them full with everything he had procured. He smiled. He felt ready to exact violent retribution on all who crossed him.

"Mr. Crossfire, you must not do this," Lazar wheezed from the floor, blood trickling down the gunsmith's forehead. "You will ruin me, condemn me to death."

Crossfire lashed out with a boot to the head, silencing Lazar once and for all.

He quickly removed his clothing and donned his new protective uniform, complete with the cross hairs logo atop the chest. He filled the belt with bullets and explosives and grabbed an Uzi. The rest remained in the bags. It was time to leave.

Crossfire slung two of the bags up, one over each shoulder, and held another two in his hands. He was now ready to take on The Wraith, ready to take on anyone that stood in his way. He sped out into the restaurant, past the babbling Oriental and out into the murky Metro City night. A cab came trundling by. Crossfire stepped out in front of it, causing the car to come to a sudden halt.

"Hey, what's the big idea?" the driver, a middle-aged blond man, yelled out the window.

Crossfire rounded the vehicle, reached in and yanked the driver out, throwing him to the street as though he was a candy wrapper being tossed into the garbage.

"HEY!" the driver screamed in protest.

Into the cab went the bags and, with Crossfire at the wheel, the car quickly disappeared into the next street.

"Metro City must pay," Crossfire said, repeating those words over and over again as he drove further into city traffic.

* * * * * *

METRO CITY - TWO YEARS EARLIER

She ambled down the street, having just left her place of employment and having rejected yet another romantic overture from one of her co-workers at the shelter, an attractive young man by the name of Mark. She just didn't feel ready to start dating. She still felt somewhat awkward mixing in society in any form, and her loss of memory, having no past whatsoever, didn't help any either. She couldn't even remember her true name, but had been using the moniker Marcia ever since she'd seen *The Brady Bunch* on television for the first time. Marcia Bradford, not wishing to copy the show too closely.

Natalya.

That name had haunted her since that awful Dr. Standish had uttered it to her more than two years prior. She had no recognition of it at all, and yet somehow it felt familiar, but the strange thing was it felt like it was something she shouldn't try to remember at all.

She had tried to recall anything else from her past. Over and over again she wrestled with her mind, attempting to wriggle anything free that might give her some indication of her previous life. But nothing worked. All the questions she had when she first woke in that Hell-hole remained—Did she have any family? What was her true name? Where had she come from? So many questions and absolutely no answers for any of them. It was true she did have some sort of accent, which would indicate she wasn't originally from the States, but opinion varied as to the origin of it, and so she always found herself back at square one.

All she knew of herself was what she had discovered from the first day of her new life. She had incredible strength, which she realized was not normal, that Dr. Standish was likely responsible for, and which terrified her. She once thought to test the limits of this strength and found she could lift one end of a car with some effort. If this was all she could lift—she wasn't yet sure—she wasn't fully game to try anything further.

There was another ability she had discovered in more recent times, quite by accident, and which was another reason she continually knocked back Mark's romantic advances. One day, when she had visited the welfare office to try and register for any kind of benefit she thought she might have been entitled to, she was able to somehow woo the office clerk despite being initially told she was ineligible due to a lack of identification, including a social security number. When she had become stressed at the lack of assistance being offered her, the clerk's demeanor instantly changed, and he was then only too eager to help in any way, including creating a new social security number for her right there on the spot. It was only with supreme effort she was able to escape without him proposing marriage to her right there and then. The incident frightened her out of her wits.

Over time, Marcia had managed to build a new life for herself and, with her newly acquired identification, was able to get out and land herself a job. Little did she realize at the time she would find it in the homeless shelter where she had first made her home in Metro.

She turned onto Fifth Street, where her car was parked, just in time to spot something ducking into an alley she knew could not possibly exist. And yet.... She rubbed her eyes. Surely she must be seeing things. Perhaps it was another power manifesting itself? She started questioning her very sanity.

No, she thought. *I know what I saw.*

Curiosity, and determination to prove she wasn't bonkers, overrode her fear, and she followed the path taken by the horrific apparition. Quietly, she edged down the darkened laneway, trying her best to avoid making any sound at all, as well as avoiding what looked and smelled like an open sewer running down the center of the path beneath and in front of her.

A subtle clattering emanated from up ahead. She slowed, tiptoed to the corner and carefully peeked around. What she saw there chilled her very soul. A group of upright, walking skeletons was gathered there, all brandishing wooden spears and shields, and forming a line as though ready to march in formation in a parade. As one turned to face her direction, she could see a dripping, bloody heart encased within its bony ribcage, and she couldn't help but gasp at the terrible sight of it. Fearing discovery, she ducked back into the shadows and began to pray for her own safety.

At that moment, sounds of a melee erupted from around the corner. Again, curiosity got the better of her and she took another peek around. A costumed man in black and blue, large glowing Eyes on his chest—no doubt The Wraith she had read about in the papers—was in mortal combat with the battalion of the dead. As he dealt with the creatures with brutal efficiency, Marcia found it all intoxicating. The strength, the courage, the heroism. She felt exhilarated by it.

In what felt like mere seconds, the battle was over. The Wraith had triumphed. Marcia inched backwards, leaned against the building wall behind her and attempted to take it all in. There was a man with great powers, as she herself had, who was using those abilities for good, to help people. To do what was right and just. She suddenly felt inspired. Could she do likewise? To somehow make up for...*something* she knew she had to atone for? She felt trepidation, too, but she knew it was something to think long and hard about.

Marcia slowly retraced her steps back toward Fifth Street. She had to get home. Had to think, had to gather her thoughts.

Yes, she considered. *I have a* lot *to think about.*

~ Chapter 14 ~

He suddenly opened his eyes as though awakening from a hideous nightmare only to quickly realize it was anything but.

Patrich Azufi came to and found himself laying in a hospital bed, hooked up to a myriad of tubes and machines, bandaged and restrained so much he could barely move an inch.

He briefly wondered if he wasn't as badly wounded as he remembered, as he felt no pain at all, but then realized he was no doubt doped up to the eyeballs with painkillers. He felt *too* good to be otherwise.

A young nurse, a pretty blonde of no more than twenty-five he estimated, came in and smiled at him. She checked his chart and whistled softly.

"You're lucky to be alive, Mr. Azufi," she said at last. "If not for your chauffeur calling the police."

Even in his doped up state, Azufi could tell she was a chatterbox. But she was a looker, too, with a body to die for.

"My injuries," Azufi uttered with some difficulty, his throat extremely dry, "how bad are they?"

"I won't lie to you," she said with a sort of bemused look on her face. "You're in bad shape. Ruptured spleen, some broken ribs, extensive bruising to your kidneys, fractured cheekbone."

The list of injuries made Azufi feel nauseous.

"But you'll live," she said. "Your wife, though..."

What?

"My...my wife?"

"Oh...I wasn't supposed to say anything. Darn you, Maggie-Grace and your mouth. Always getting you into trouble. Been that way since I was a young girl back in Kansas. My momma always said my mouth would get me into trouble, cause a world of hurt. Heavens was she right."

"My wife..." Azufi whispered. "What do you mean about my wife?"

Maggie-Grace leaned down close to him. She smelled good, like flowers and candy all rolled up into one. "We weren't supposed to say anything to you until the doctors thought you were stronger, but I've let the cat out of the bag, haven't I. Your wife was brought in last night just after you were admitted. She's in a critical condition."

Azufi's heart sank, but somehow the vision of this angel before him significantly lessened the pain.

"You better be prepared for the worst," she gravely said.

* * * * * *

Crossfire eluded me again, though he's badly wounded. Have you any sight of him or knowledge of his whereabouts? - W

Sloan read the text message on his cell phone with some intensity. He and Perez stood inside a dilapidated Chinese restaurant, an elderly Chinese woman squawking about them in an unintelligible language, a covered stretcher rolling by them carrying the body of the most infamous weapons master the world had ever known. Could there be a connection between Crossfire and Lazar? Surely that was not only possible but highly likely. He texted his thoughts on the matter back to The Wraith as quickly as his fingers could type.

A reply was quick in coming, signed with a W as was The Wraith's habit.

Is Lazar's workroom largely devoid of weaponry? - W

Sloan replied in the affirmative.

He's heavily armed and out there plotting revenge. We must find him! - W

No kidding, Sloan thought, but kept that to himself.

Perez sidled up to him. "Reports of a wrecked car a few blocks from here. Might be connected with Lazar's murder."

"It's worth checking out," Sloan said.

As Perez moved over to speak with a uniformed officer, Sloan started tapping into his phone once again. *Car, Crossfire, few blocks away.*

If a bug found attached to the rear bumper, remove and destroy it. I'll be in touch - W

Sloan smiled, put his phone back into his pocket. It was good to know they had each other's back. Good to know they were now working together for the common good, that The Wraith was someone he could trust with his life and then some.

"Okay, Perez," Sloan said. "Let's go check out that wreck."

* * * * * *

The Wraith slammed his cell phone back into his belt in frustration. Not only had Crossfire managed to escape once again, but he had also re-equipped himself with the weapons of war. No doubt the villain was readying to wage just such a war. The only minor consolation The Wraith could figure into all this was the death of Lazar. At least Crossfire would be unable to re-arm once his current stockpile was exhausted. But the damage he could do in the meantime was unfathomable. He had to shut down his foe once and for all. But how? How?

He majestically stood atop a skyscraper roof, his cape catching the breeze, trying to ascertain what Crossfire's next—and his own—move would be.

His hideout has been compromised, The Wraith mulled over, *his links to Azufi have been uncovered. Either location would now be off limits to him. So, even taking his madness into account, he would have to find another hole in which to hide while he formulates his plan of action. I need to stop him before he can do anything else against me. Against this city.*

Despite losing his quarry once again, The Wraith refused to become dispirited. He knew full well he was the only one who stood between Crossfire and his insane plans for revenge. There had to be some way to anticipate Crossfire's next move, to find him before another attack could be launched.

All might be lost if he was to fail.

* * * * * *

Crossfire eased into the hotel room, the very same room he had stayed in months earlier when he had first arrived in town, and fell onto the bed. He was badly wounded and he could barely see out of one eye, which had largely swollen shut. He was of no use to anyone right now. He needed to rest, to try and make sense of his rambling thoughts. But he was tired. So very tired. He still intended to make The Wraith pay for all his infractions. His vendetta was not yet complete.

He pulled the gold coin from his pocket, twirled it in his fingers while constantly staring at it. Even after he had returned the coin to the town elders in Karbah years before, he found he couldn't be separated from it for long. He asked for it back and, while he remained in the village, the elders were only too willing to oblige. But now...

Rest didn't come easy; his mind and body felt an unease he couldn't control. He sat up and eyed the bags filled with his equipment by the door in front of him. He didn't know how, but he would make the city pay for allowing The Wraith to roam its streets without question. Without consequence.

Well, there would be consequences now, Crossfire thought. *It's too late for this city to be redeemed.*

It had to pay dearly for its transgressions. And Crossfire now knew what he had to do. All had become clear.

He would allow himself more time to rest and heal, but time was also of the essence. His mission, his vendetta, needed to be seen through. Nothing would stop him.

Metro City was doomed.

* * * * * *

"The car's registered as stolen," Perez announced. "Forensics tells us it's full of prints, but we'll have to wait for the test results for any identification."

"If they're Crossfire's, we won't know it. His prints aren't on file."

Sloan lifted his cap, looked up into the night sky. It was chilly and overcast, but there were still a few stars visible. The streets were largely deserted save for a handful of winos milling about, their desolate misery interrupted briefly by the police activity.

He circled the wreck and examined it closely from all sides. The front end was completely smashed in, with a lengthy gash along the passenger side. The driver's side door was open. There was nothing of note inside the vehicle, no clue left behind by its occupant save a series of prints. At the rear, Sloan saw what he was after. He bent over and removed from the bumper a small bug planted there by The Wraith. He discreetly placed it into his pocket without anyone, especially Perez, noticing.

"Well, what do we do now?" Perez asked, hands on hips.

"Back to the station," Sloan replied. "I have this gut feeling we're missing something. I want to go through everything we know about the case. There must be something in the file that can help us. I feel sure we've overlooked something."

"If you say so," Perez said, rolling her eyes. "But I'd just as soon head home and get at least two or three hours sleep."

"C'mon," Sloan said. "Sleep can wait. We have work to do."

* * * * * *

Azufi dozed comfortably in his hospital bed. He smiled and stretched a little, feeling the soft cotton sheets on his arms. He still felt no pain, ensuring his attendants kept him healthily doped up at all times. He was currently in that strange half asleep, half awake zone in which he was clearly dreaming but *knew* it to be a dream, while also semi-aware of his hospital surroundings.

Turning over to get more comfortable, he smiled again as he recognized Maggie-Grace's perfume. His favorite nurse had obviously entered the room. Maybe he should try and chat her up?

"Wakey wakey," a harsh and somewhat familiar voice grated.

Azufi's eyes burst open. There he caught sight of the man who had brutally beaten him the night before, mere hours ago, in fact. Marcus Redding of the Bandidos biker gang. The biker's long red hair now flowed freely, cascading around his ears and face. His expression was one of anger and stubbornness. He held Maggie-Grace firmly in his arms, a hand over her mouth.

"Good," Marcus said. "I need you awake so you can tell me what I need to know."

"What...are you...talking about?" Azufi struggled to say, his throat constantly parched.

"Word on the street is you're not completely in control of your business. You're not really calling the shots over there. Who is? Where can I find him?"

"I don't know," Azufi said softly, sweat beginning to trickle down his forehead.

"Talk fast," Marcus ordered, gritting his yellow-stained teeth and gripping Maggie-Grace tighter by her throat, "or this beautiful young thing won't be so beautiful anymore." She whimpered a little.

What do I care? Azufi thought. *I don't know her.*

"Then I'll turn my attention to you," Marcus said. "Finish what I started last night."

"All I know is his name...Crossfire," Azufi finally relented, his sense of self-preservation coming to the fore. "*He* took out Latham, forced me to do what he said. I don't know where he is or what he's now doing, but there's one thing I *do* know..."

Azufi coughed and sputtered, trying to get some moisture into his throat.

"...he's after The Wraith, has some sort of mad vendetta against him."

Marcus stood rigid, letting his grip on Maggie-Grace slacken a little. He was clearly contemplating all he had been told. After a moment or so, he let go of the nurse and bolted from the room, letting the door slam shut behind him.

Maggie-Grace, tears streaming down her face, quickly moved over to Azufi's bed and sat down beside him, clearly relieved and grateful to him.

"Oh, Mr. Azufi," she said, crying. "You saved my life. However can I thank you?"

Azufi smiled subtly, took a deep breath, enjoying her scent, enjoying being so close to someone so young and sexy.

"I'm sure we can think of something," he said at last.

~ Chapter 15 ~

Sloan poured through a portion of the file that lay open before him on his desk, while Perez did likewise through the digital files on her computer at her desk. Anything to do with the Latham/Grieco murders, the latter's prison escape, the attacks on the city, any eyewitness testimonies, Sloan wanted everything perused yet again for anything that might have been missed. He felt sure there was something, but couldn't quite put his finger on it. His hunches were rarely wrong.

Suddenly, he stumbled across some information. A little something, perhaps less than that even, but he knew it was potentially worth pursuing. He sat forward in his chair, his eyes narrowing as he considered its possible significance.

"Found something?" Perez, ever observant, asked.

"Umm...no...nothing really. I was just thinking the case over. You?"

"Nothing's standing out to me so far, though there's still a lot to read. But we've gone through these files at least three times already. I don't see how it's possible we could have overlooked anything. It's late. Why don't we go home and get a little rest. A couple of hours aren't going to affect the case anyway," Perez said.

Sloan stood. "I gotta go to the john and pee. Keep at it, we're not done yet."

Perez sighed as he passed her and headed for the washroom. Once there, Sloan locked himself in a stall and began typing on his cell:

Found something you might be interested in. A cab driver I've suspected was murdered by Crossfire. An eyewitness claims to have seen the cab parked at a fleabag hotel—the Pembleton Arms—days before the driver's body was found. It's a long shot in regards to Crossfire's current location, but it might be something to look into all the same - Sloan

A response was fast in coming.

Well done. I'll head there immediately. Wait to hear from me - W

Wait? Wait for what? Sloan thought. *I'm heading out there ASAP. If there's even a remote chance Crossfire's there now, I want in on the capture.*

He marched from his stall, with fellow officers giving him funny looks as he went, and out into the precinct proper.

"Let's go, Perez," he called out to his partner. "I've maybe got us a lead, but we have to get there fast. It's clear across town."

"What?" Perez said, clearly confused. "But you were just peeing?"

Sloan had to practically yank her from her chair and drag her outside to his car. "C'mon. We don't want to be late."

* * * * * *

The Wraith guided his Rolls into the Pembleton Arms parking lot. It was an expansive area, largely empty, save for a few beat up cars here and there. He craned his vision up the ten or so storeys that made up the fancily-named, but shabby in reality, hotel. There was no light visible at the rear of the building, which wasn't much of a surprise at 4:30AM. Whatever the time, the utmost caution always had to be maintained where Crossfire was concerned.

"I've hacked into the hotel's booking system, Chief," Max said via the car's comm link. "There's a guest called Jack Sun staying in room 523. Fifth floor, rear. It's the only name that sounds promising."

Jack Sun, The Wraith thought. *Clever. For Jackson Thomas, Crossfire's real name, the one and only piece of information we've ever been able to ascertain about the man's past. He's wiped all records of that past from every database I've thought to look through. Only Crossfire exists now.*

"I hate that you're going in alone," Max said. "Leena and I should be out with you. If Crossfire's there..."

"There wasn't time, Max," The Wraith said. "I'm hoping, with the element of surprise again on my side, coupled with Crossfire's injuries, that I should be able to take him down quickly and effectively. Wish me luck."

"Always."

He exited the car and checked the equipment in his belt. Fully stocked, everything in order and ready to go. He was about to produce his grapnel gun from his belt when a series of mighty explosions ripped through the hotel, the force of which sent The Wraith pummeling back, slamming into the side of the car. He grunted in pain, but was otherwise okay. The same could not be said for the Pembleton Arms, which was beginning to topple as a fiery inferno raged on the floors above. The Wraith took a few steps back.

In seconds, the hotel was gone. Before The Wraith could even make sense of what had just happened, a further series of explosions could be heard throughout the city, three, perhaps four.

Oh no, The Wraith thought. *Crossfire truly intends on destroying Metro City!*

* * * * * *

"Crossfire!" Marcus shouted to his men. "Who the hell is Crossfire?"

Back in the Bandidos clubhouse, Marcus had convened a meeting with his men to discuss their next course of action. The rest of the gang members either replied in the negative or merely shrugged their shoulders.

"We need to find out," Marcus relayed. "He's the one running the show over at the Latham organization. He's the one who ordered the hit on us here in our safe haven. He's the one responsible for the death of my wife!"

The gang roared their anger and disapproval at that.

"Someone in this city must know who he is. *Where* he is. I don't care how long it takes or who we have to go through to get this information, but get it we will. If we have to kill every lowlife in this city to get to this bastard, so be it!"

A younger member of the gang seated at the back and by a window yawned and vacantly gazed out while Marcus continued with his speech.

"Hank!" Marcus shouted. "Pay attention."

"Sorry, Marcus," Hank said, "but come look at this weirdo outside."

Marcus, annoyed, nevertheless moved over to the window and peered out. Across the street stood a muscular, strangely outfitted man. He waved to the gang members, smiling broadly. It was hard to see, but Marcus felt sure there was a cross hairs logo on the man's tunic. "Crossfire," Marcus breathed heavily.

Crossfire held up something in his hands, showing it off to Marcus and those gang members able to see.

Is that...is that a detonator? Marcus thought, his blood freezing.

That thought was Marcus's last. Crossfire twisted the device in his hands, then there was a bright flash, then darkness.

* * * * * *

"What was that, Perez?" Sloan barked, slamming his foot on the brakes, bringing his beat up car to a screeching halt mid traffic.

"Holy..." Perez could only offer in response. A giant plume of flame and smoke spewed upward above the skyline in front of them. "Look." She pointed into the rear view mirror.

Sloan quickly turned in his seat, where the same sight greeted them in the direction they had just come.

"What the hell?" Sloan bitterly muttered. A few seconds and he regained his composure. "Call it in, Perez, we need emergency crews out here pronto."

As his partner did so, Sloan exited the car and glanced at his watch. Nearly 6AM. Dawn would be breaking soon. And with it, slowly but surely, would come the peak hour traffic. People would begin to flood into the city by car, train, and by foot, all making their way to work as they always did.

Sloan realized they would need to prevent that from happening. The city was currently under attack so the fewer civilians affected the better. They would need every man and woman on the job to try and deflect people from entering the inner city.

"Fire and ambulance are out and massing, but they're all under staffed as you know," Perez said. "But there's something else—I can't get through to headquarters."

Sloan felt the blood draining from his face as he heard that. The explosion behind them, coming from the direction they had come from. Could it...could it be?

"Nobody is answering," she said.

* * * * * *

The Wraith stood atop the nearest skyscraper and surveyed the city skyline. There had been at least four other massive explosions, he estimated. He tried to get a closer look with his binoculars, tried to identify the buildings affected. Latham Industries was the most obvious casualty. Metro City's tallest structure was now largely no more. Two buildings within close proximity to each other had been hit within the very heart of the city, and while he couldn't make sure which from his current vantage point, he had a strong suspicion as to their identity. The Pembleton Arms Hotel lay behind him and there had been another blast off to the west.

The Dread Avenger felt a mixture of horror and intense fury. Crossfire would pay dearly for this, he vowed. He would offer his enemy no mercy.

"Darling," Leena's voice came over the comm link in The Wraith's cowl, "are you all right?"

"I'm fine," The Wraith said swiftly, "but what can you report of the attacks? Can you relay what's been hit?"

"As far as MNN is reporting, City Hall and Police Headquarters have been wiped out as has Latham Industries. Wait a minute...they're just getting word that the city hospital has been as well." Leena's shaky and almost teary voice made his heart ache. He would love to be there to comfort here, but duty called.

"You can add the Pembleton Arms Hotel to that list," The Wraith grimly said.

He let his arms drop. Never before had he felt this helpless, this despondent as he did at that moment. He had failed. Failed his city, failed those untold masses that had been brutally slaughtered by Crossfire.

Another explosion tore him from his thoughts, adding to the cacophony of despair that had become Metro City. This one was further west than the previous. It looked as though it was in that direction Crossfire was now headed. But what was worth destroying out west, at least from Crossfire's point of view? To the west, beyond the inner city precinct lay the boroughs and neighborhoods where Metro's middle and lower classes made their homes. There was nothing of significance there for Crossfire to use to make any sort of statement against the city.

Then it hit home, and The Wraith damned his slow wittedness. There was definitely a building, an area of immense importance out west.

Melton Memorial Airport.

~ Chapter 16 ~

"He's heading west to the airport," The Wraith said over his in-cowl comm link. "Max, you and Leena head out there. Make sure Leena is fully outfitted and prepared in her new suit. I'll try and get whatever police is left heading there as well. Whatever it takes to take Crossfire down. Out."

He leapt into his Rolls and gunned the engine to life. He didn't know if he'd be able to overtake Crossfire and reach the airport before him, but he didn't intend letting anyone else die this night.

Whatever it takes...it ends tonight!

* * * * * *

Leena looked to Max with some trepidation. "Is the suit ready? I didn't think you'd completed testing it."

"No, but it'll be fine," Max said with his usual confident flair. "And what better way to test it than out there in the field? C'mon, let's get you suited up. We haven't a moment to lose."

* * * * * *

The Wraith pushed his car to the limit, careening through traffic with the pinpoint accuracy of a NASCAR driver. As he neared a site of devastation, all around showed evidence of Crossfire's carnage. Crowds of people billowed onto the sidewalks, rushing to escape the destruction. Cars, too, bustled this way and that, impeding The Wraith's progress in this portion of the city.

With his horn blaring, and zigzagging left and right, The Wraith managed to slice through the crowds, but time was lost. He only hoped he would not be too late. He felt sure Crossfire was headed for the airport, but how much of a head start the villain had on him he could only guess.

As he swerved the Rolls around a sharp bend, avoiding much of the surge of people, The Wraith noticed a series of smashed cars strewn about the street up ahead. He slammed a foot on the gas and sped forward. Injured drivers and their passengers crawled out of their vehicles or stood about in shock. Clearly someone had crashed through this area and The Wraith knew who it was.

The damage here is only recent, The Wraith thought. *Despite my brief delay, I must be gaining on Crossfire.*

As he piled on the speed, a large gas tanker loomed in the distance, veering left and right.

Crossfire! It's got to be.

The Wraith pressed on, gaining on the tanker, the driver of which appeared intent on causing as much damage as possible. A few minutes more, and The Wraith was riding the tanker's rear. The truck suddenly picked up speed, although it continued careening left and right. The Wraith desperately tried to pull his Rolls up alongside it, but the tanker blocked him at every opportunity.

When the tanker next pulled to the right, The Wraith instantly gunned his car to the left, moving into position next to the speeding truck. They hurtled through the city as though locked into position, each keeping pace with the other.

The Wraith took a moment to glance to his right, saw Crossfire at the wheel of the truck glancing back at him. The look of insane fury on the villain's face spoke volumes. Crossfire yanked at his wheel, slamming the truck into the Rolls. The Wraith hung on for dear life and managed to remain in control of his racing vehicle without a loss of momentum.

The Dread Avenger knew he couldn't maintain this position for long. Eventually the tanker would bash his Rolls into submission, and Crossfire would escape to continue his reign of terror on the city. He also couldn't race up ahead and pull out in front of the truck. The result would be the same. No, The Wraith knew what had to be done—he had to get onboard the truck itself and deal with Crossfire personally. It was the only way.

"Autopilot, engage," The Wraith said. A blue light flashed on the dashboard. "After I exit, maintain pursuit of adjacent truck."

"Understood," an electronic voice rung out from within the Rolls.

The tanker was beginning to pull ahead. It was now or never. The Wraith eased his way into the passenger seat and opened the door. He found himself adjacent to the tanker's rear trailer. Without another second wasted, he leapt over and latched onto the steel ladder at the trailer's rear. He craned his vision backward and saw the Rolls glide in behind the truck, sticking to it like glue.

There wasn't another moment to lose. As the tanker continued its high speed journey through the city streets, The Wraith lithely climbed the ladder and carefully scurried atop the trailer toward the truck's cabin. The flurry of wind caused his cape to cascade outward, but nothing would deter The Wraith from the task at hand.

In one swift, deft move, he dropped down onto the truck's passenger foot plate and an instant later opened the door, bustling inside.

"You!" Crossfire madly cried. "Always you!"

The final battle for the fate of Metro City began as The Wraith let loose with a series of punches to Crossfire's face while attempting to wrestle control of the truck at the same time. Crossfire, in turn, replied with a series of punches and knees to the head. It was a vicious assault, neither willing to yield and, as the tanker continued its mad thrust toward the airport, the battle waged on.

"Gonna kill you," Crossfire spat. "Kill you!"

Blow after powerful blow was traded as they ferociously wrestled. Tires screeched and The Wraith looked up. The truck plowed through a high wire fence, its speed not checked in the slightest. The Wraith groaned inwardly, realizing they had reached the airport and were now whizzing toward the various runways ahead of them. Beyond those lay the expansive terminals and parked airplanes, glowing like a series of Christmas trees before them.

A savage knee to the face caught The Wraith off guard, stunning him back into the passenger seat.

"Gonna kill us all," Crossfire declared. "Gonna kill as many as possible."

The Wraith, his head spinning, his vision blurred, nevertheless noted Crossfire pointing the tanker straight for the parked planes far up ahead. This terrible reality shook him back to his senses. He again wildly grappled with Crossfire, battling not only for his own life, but for those of untold innocents nearby.

"I won't...let you...do this," The Wraith grunted as the countless planes grew in size, looming larger and larger in the windshield of the truck.

As they wrestled, The Wraith connected with a mighty elbow to Crossfire's nose. The resulting sickening crack indicated he had shattered Crossfire's nasal septum. The villain shrieked in agony. The Wraith finally gained control of the tanker as a result. Tightly gripping the wheel, a massive 747 parked just before them, The Wraith jerked the wheel sharply to the left, simultaneously slamming a foot on the brakes. The truck's wheels seized and the truck convulsed and jack-knifed, skidding closer and closer to the hapless plane. The Wraith couldn't bear to look. He had done all he could. But was it enough?

Then silence.

He slowly opened his eyes and allowed the joyous sight of crisis averted to fill his senses. He had managed to stop the truck mere inches from the plane.

His joy and relief was short-lived as Crossfire lashed out with a brutal kick, sending The Wraith pummeling from the tanker and crashing onto the tarmac below. Crossfire, blood gushing from his nose, quickly stood over him.

"You may have saved all of them," Crossfire said, waving toward the plane and adjacent terminal, "but after I'm through with you, I'll take 'em all out. All of 'em, you hear me. All of 'em!"

"Not this day," a female voice rang out.

Crossfire whirled, revealing to The Wraith Leena, outfitted as Lady Wraith, with fierce determination writ large upon her handsome features.

Before Crossfire could make sense of what was happening, Lady Wraith activated her Eyes of Judgment. The Wraith narrowly averted his eyes; the blinding light caused Crossfire to stagger backwards.

"Aargh!" the villain moaned. "My eyes. What have you done to me?" Crossfire helplessly flailed about.

"Don't worry," Lady Wraith said, "you won't be in pain much longer."

She let fly with a spinning scissor kick, connecting perfectly with Crossfire's head. He fell to the ground with a thud. Despite his injuries, Crossfire remained defiant, clawing his way up and to his knees.

"No, Crossfire," The Wraith said firmly, "this truly ends now. Metro City will never fall to the likes of you. Never!" He lashed out with a kick of his own. Crossfire fell face forward, unconscious.

The war was over.

The Dread Avenger looked over to his partner; a mix of relief and gratitude flooded his heart. The battle was won. Metro City and its people were safe. But at what cost? Wraith gazed to the heavens. Countless lives lost, a city panicked and partially destroyed. Its economy, with the murder of Robert Latham, was in tatters. So much pain and sorrow...

Lady Wraith placed a reassuring and calming hand on his shoulder, nudging him back to the issue at hand.

"Here," he said. "Place these restraints around Crossfire's wrists. I'll leave this as a signal to Sloan. He should be here soon."

She did so, while The Wraith attached a small card, emblazoned with the symbol of the Eyes of Judgment, to the villain's shirt.

"Quickly now," he said. "Into the Rolls. I can already hear the emergency vehicles approaching. Our job here is done."

They sprinted for the Rolls parked nearby, and they were soon off into the night.

* * * * * *

Bob Sloan sat on his couch at home, flipping a paper card over in his right hand. It was nearly daybreak, but he wasn't in the mood for sleep. Not after the night he just had. Not after what the city had just been through. He looked down at the card in his hand, noted what it represented. He briefly smiled.

A beep indicated an incoming message on his cell.

Is Crossfire safely incarcerated? - W

Sloan quickly replied in the affirmative. Crossfire was safely ensconced within the confines of the Metro City Asylum, and would likely be transferred to Guantanamo Bay, classified as an enemy of the state, never to be released.

He leaned back on the couch and mulled over recent events. The city had been through so much lately, this dark mood and now Crossfire's war on everything. So many people gone, so many good cops amongst them.

Another beep from his cell brought him back to the present.

Take heart, friend Sloan. This city has lost many, has seen its fair share of pain and tragedy. But good has triumphed over evil. As it always will as long as there is breath in my body – W

He's right, Sloan thought. *We must never give up the fight. Good must always triumph over evil.*

He smiled again.

Don't worry, my friend, he typed. *Your fight against such evil will never be in vain. And you are never alone in your struggle.*

The battle for the fate of Metro City was a never-ending one, it seemed. But it was a battle that would never be fought alone.

~ Epilogue ~

The cries of the insane wound horribly and inexorably through the maze of corridors that constituted the Metro City Asylum. As the myriad care workers and maintenance staff went about their daily duties, attempting to drown out the horrendous din all around them, one padded cell in the institution's most guarded quarter was conspicuous in its silence.

* * * * * *

Inside, a newly added inmate, securely trussed up in a straitjacket that was latched to the wall, sat Crossfire. He rocked back and forth slightly and silently on his cot, his mind racing with thoughts of violence and revenge.

I'm coming to my senses, he thought, *I'm not insane. I'll show 'em, show 'em all. I'm not insane, I don't belong here. One day I'll get out. I'll show 'em all I'm not insane. I'll kill 'em. Kill 'em all!*

"You hear that?" he suddenly shouted at the top of his lungs. "I'll get out of here one day. You'll see. I'm not insane. I AM NOT INSANE! MY VENDETTA IS NOT YET COMPLETE!"

He felt the spittle running down his mouth and chin, but he didn't care. He returned to his silent rocking, content in the knowledge he was not insane and would soon prove that to the world.

And to The Wraith.

* * * * * *

With the moon semi-full in the night-sky above, the ruins of the Latham Estate lay before him, a horrific mess of brick and timber. The once expansive house was no more, merely a pile of moldering debris that was unrecognizable as the once mighty and proud home of Robert Latham. Weeds began to protrude here and there, adding to the sense of decay and utter desolation.

As he trudged through the wreckage, a breeze curled around him, causing the dust and dirt to rise in a haze. He found it hard for his cane to gain purchase on the uneven ground, the steel ferrule sliding back and forth, bumping against brick and concrete. He kicked at an oversized chunk of gravel in frustration and almost lost his footing in the process. He gingerly clutched at his left leg.

"I swear, by all that I hold dear," he finally said with a wheeze, "that I will rebuild. All this and more will return to its former glory. I will come back bigger and stronger than ever!"

He turned from the house and wistfully gazed at the overgrown grounds of his former estate. Even in the darkness of night, with the dim light of the moon and the glow of the city beyond, he could see the devastation wrought upon his former stronghold.

"That fool Azufi couldn't handle an organization like this. Or enemies like Crossfire or The Wraith. Only Robert Latham can. And will. I *will* return and I *will* wreak unmitigated harm upon all that oppose me." Latham smirked at the thought of his return to glory. "Nobody beats Robert Latham and lives!"

He turned and slowly limped back to an awaiting limousine down the drive from his former home. He *would* return, and soon. When the time was ripe, when all the pieces were in place, his plans would then be put into inevitable motion. To reclaim his kingdom.

Soon. *Very* soon.

* * * * * *

The Wraith silently crouched atop a city skyscraper, his right hand touching at his temple, Lady Wraith huddled by his side.

"Anything?" she enquired.

"The bug attached to the coin is working just fine," The Wraith replied. "Crossfire thinks he's getting better, thinks he's fine and will soon escape his confines. But with the coin secreted in his cell, his total and unrecoverable insanity is assured."

"As is his immortality."

The Wraith turned to face his partner. "Yes. Perhaps one day we can discreetly remove the coin. But for now, a sane, composed Jackson Thomas is not what we need. At least this way, he'll be completely incapable of escape as his mind drifts further and further into incoherence. As tragic as this is...it's for the best."

Sadness drifted over Lady Wraith's visage, but also a firm resoluteness The Wraith knew all too well. He smiled at her.

"Shall we continue our patrol?" he said.

"Lead on," she replied.

They stood and turned when suddenly a bright light, which seemed to come from nowhere and everywhere all at once, blocked their path. A raging storm built up, a ferocious wind caused their capes to tightly wrap around their bodies. Electrical bolts shot this way and that, and quickly, a small black circle appeared in the air before them. It grew and grew. An instant later, three faint, shadowy forms could be seen within, and then...

The light and wind disappeared as swiftly as it had come, replaced by three forms standing ahead of them. One was outfitted from head-to-toe in shining armor, like a knight from the days of old, brandishing a blueish-tinted sword. Alongside him was a lady shrouded in mist, dressed in white frilly lace, floating slightly above the roof of the building. Her lustrous blonde hair cascaded about her face as though a breeze fluttered through it. And next to her was...was...

Natalya Blackova?

"You are The Wraith?" the knight barked at them, his voice deep and assured.

"Who are you?" The Wraith asked in return. "What is all this? And do you realize whom you have with you?" He pointed at Blackova, whom he noticed to have a completely blank and innocent expression.

"There is no time for explanations," the misty lady breathed, her melodic voice echoing from every corner. "I am the Lady of the Lake. And you, Wraith and Lady Wraith, are needed to combat a deadly threat to this planet. All life on Earth is at stake. You must come with us now."

A look of trepidation and consternation crossed Lady Wraith's features. The Wraith knew well how she felt. Before he could reply, the Lady of the Lake reached gracefully forward with an arm, and with the snap of her fingers... they were all gone.

TO BE CONTINUED...

~ Author's Note ~

This story really came out of nowhere. I'd been trying to complete the intended next book in the series, *Swamp Witch of Satan's Forest,* for some length of time, but the entire story never really coalesced in my mind. While I do still mean to finish that story, though as a series of shorts for inclusion in an anthology or perhaps as an extra in a future Wraith novel, the idea of *Vendetta*—bringing the villainous Crossfire back to taunt our vaunted hero—fired my imagination. Once that central notion came to me, the novel almost wrote itself. I'm very pleased with it and I hope you enjoyed it.

Writing can be an incredible joy, but it can also be a major pain. Not just finding the time to actually do it, in amongst my day job and life's other chores, but once you've actually committed to writing the piece, it begins to consume you. Every waking moment, whether you're actively working on it at that point or not, is filled with thoughts on the work. Ideas on how to proceed, what action scenes to include, who lives or dies, where and when it all takes place, how to finish it all off. It all bashes around in your head, day and night, until the work is completed, when relief is finally at hand. And satisfaction at a job (hopefully) well done.

As with every story I write, it's the culmination of a lot of hard work which many people, to varying degrees, contributed to, and I'd like to thank them all here.

To my wife Jennifer: thank you again for everything you have given me. Love, companionship, friendship and so much more. The Wraith (and myself) would be nothing without you. To my family, who is, and always has been, there for me...I cannot thank you enough. Thanks also to my team at Trinity Comics—Jeff Welborn, Roland Bird, Jeff Austin, Adam O. Pruett, Rick Hannah and Splash!—you guys are the best; and to my editor, AP Fuchs, for helping craft this piece into what it is.

And to you, my dear and loyal readers, thank you once again for taking The Wraith into your hearts. I can only hope that I continue to live up to your high expectations of my work and continue to deliver on those expectations. It is for you that I do what I do. It's a passion project, and I hope that shows in the work. So again, from my heart to yours, thanks.

The next book to be released will be either *Book Two* in the *Books of Judgment, Serpent Rising!* (featuring the full origin of the villainous Cobra, himself. Who is he, how did he become the master of pain, the Moriarty to The Wraith's Holmes? All will be revealed in *Serpent Rising*, co-written by myself and Greg Gick, coming soon); or *Kingdom*, #6 in *The Wraith Adventures* series. More on all that soon.

For now, relax and take heart that there is plenty more to come in the world of The Wraith Dread Avenger of the Underworld.

Take care.

Frank Dirscherl
Wollongong, 2018

About the Type

Garamond is a group of many old-style serif typefaces, originally those designed by Parisian craftsman Claude Garamond and other 16th century French engravers, and now many modern revivals. Though his name was written as 'Garamont' in his lifetime, the typefaces are generally spelled 'Garamond'. **Garamond-Normal**, used in this book, is one of those modern revivals.

~ Also Available ~

a Wraith Adventures tale

SANDERSON OF METRO

Frank Dirscherl & Bobby Nash

Two masters of the pulp fiction world, Frank Dirscherl and Bobby
Nash, have come together to tell this tale, the secret NEVER before
told origin of the first Wraith/Paul Sanderson, as only they could.
This action-packed, atmospheric thrill could only be told now, and
it could only be told by master storytellers like Dirscherl and
Nash. An epic never to be repeated and not to be missed.
ISBN: 978-0-646-97923-6

AVAILABLE NOW!

www.trinitycomics.com

The Wraith Adventures #1
THE WRAITH: SPECIAL EDITION
Frank Dirscherl

Celebrating the character's twentieth anniversary. The original
novel now features a new author preface, interview with the
author, a sketchbook featuring never before seen art by Jim Taylor,
Jeff Austin, Roland Bird and John Jett and sneak peeks at the
novels *Valley of Evil* and *Vendetta*.
ISBN: 978-0-646-98436-0

AVAILABLE NOW!

www.trinitycomics.com

The Wraith Adventures #2
VALLEY OF EVIL
Frank Dirscherl

After the horror the Cobra unleashed upon Metro City, Paul
Sanderson has recuperated, regained his strength and focus, and
the city has been rebuilt while its citizens have slowly started to
regroup and move forward. Into this relative calm marches Ma Tzi,
the Hong Kong drug lord, who senses a weakness in resident crime
lord Robert Latham's hold on the city and intends to exploit that
in any way necessary. And at any cost.
ISBN: 978-0-646-90809-0

AVAILABLE NOW!
www.trinitycomics.com

The Wraith Adventures #2.5
CROSSFIRE
Stephen J. Semones; edited by Frank Dirscherl

After a terrorist attack leaves the citizens of Metro City reeling, an
enigmatic stranger emerges from the wake of the destruction to
wage war on local crime-lord Robert Latham. In the midst of this,
Max Horton, The Wraith's right-hand man, vanishes without a
trace. Searching for Max, and for those responsible for the
devastation, The Wraith sets out for answers.
ISBN: 978-0-646-58377-8

AVAILABLE NOW!

The Wraith Adventures #3
CULT OF THE DAMNED
Frank Dirscherl

With the city back firmly in his grasp, crime lord and entrepreneur
Robert Latham is celebrating by bankrolling Metro City's 200th
anniversary gala year, which includes the unveiling of a never-
before-seen ancient Aztec stone carving—the Cortes Stone—at the
City Gallery, a carving that has thrilled the scientific and artistic
communities, but infuriated the monstrous Aztekoth.
ISBN: 978-0-646-90824-3

AVAILABLE NOW!

The Wraith Adventures #4
CRY OF THE WEREWOLF
Frank Dirscherl

Having gone through ordeal after ordeal, Paul Sanderson (aka The Wraith Dread Avenger of the Underworld ®) and his love Leena Patterson, decide to take a long overdue vacation. However, their idyll is soon shattered by an attack by a creature nobody thought could possibly exist—a werewolf. Soon, an evil so heinous makes himself known, and only The Wraith could possibly defeat it.
ISBN: 978-0-646-57757-9

AVAILABLE NOW!

www.trinitycomics.com

Join FRANK DIRSCHERL and Trinity
Comics on social media!

facebook.com/publisherTrinityComics

@Trinity_Comics

instagram.com/trinity.comics

trinitycomics.proboards.com

All Trinity Comics, The Wraith, Starflame and
Global Protectors novels, comics and merchandise
can be obtained directly from the Trinity Comics
website – www.trinitycomics.com

Want to be The Wraith?

Well, it might be hard to actually *be* The Wraith, unless of course you, too, have been endowed with the power of the Eyes of Judgment. But you can certainly dress, drink and drive like him [*] (and you don't always have to be a millionaire to do so). See for yourselves.

The Wraith/Paul Sanderson wears:

- tailored clothing from Cad & the Dandy Tailors and Shirtmakers – www.cadandthedandy.co.uk
- bespoke footwear from Gaziano & Girling – www.gazianogirling.com
- watches from Tudor (Tudor Heritage Black Bay Bay Blue) www.tudorwatch.com
- Armani Code cologne from Giorgio Armani – www.giorgioarmanibeauty-usa.com/for-him-armani-code/for-him-armani-code,default,sc.html

drinks:

- Twinings Earl & Lady Grey tea – www.twinings.co.uk
- Keurig coffee – www.keurig.com/
- The Balvenie Scotch whisky – www.thebalvenie.com
- Armand de Brignac champagne – www.armanddebrignac.com
- Cosmopolitan cocktails

---

[*] Please note: Trinity Comics does not condone drinking and driving. **All** adults, please always drink responsibly and never drink and drive

uses:

- Dell laptops - www.dell.com.au
- Chesterfield furniture from Abbey Furniture
  www.chesterfieldfurnituremelbourne.com.au
- wallets from Launer - www.launer.com
- a Samsung Galaxy J5 Pro cell phone -
  www.samsung.com/latin_en/smartphones/galaxy-j5-2017/SM-
  J530GZDITPA/

drives:

- a Rolls Royce Wraith - www.rolls-roycemotorcars.com/en-
  GB/wraith.html

And, if you're really eager to actually look like The Wraith—in full costume—then you can always head over to Xtreme Design FX and let Lance Coulter there make you an exact replica of the costume used for The Wraith motion picture - www.xtremedesignfx.com